Eddie's Luck

Eddie's Luck

Kathleen Stevens

Atheneum · 1992 · New York

Maxwell Macmillan Canada
Toronto

Maxwell Macmillan International
New York   Oxford   Singapore   Sydney

Atheneum
Macmillan Publishing Company
866 Third Avenue
New York, NY 10022

Maxwell Macmillan Canada, Inc.
1200 Eglinton Avenue East
Suite 200
Don Mills, Ontario M3C 3N1

Macmillan Publishing Company is part of the Maxwell Communication
Group of Companies.

First edition

Printed in the United States of America

10 9 8 7 6 5 4 3 2 1

The text of this book is set in 12/15½ Times Roman.

Library of Congress Cataloging-in-Publication Data
Stevens, Kathleen.
Eddie's luck / by Kathleen Stevens.—1st ed.
p.   cm.
Summary: Eleven-year-old Eddie is dismayed to have to share his room with his
eighty-three-year-old grandfather while he recovers from a stroke, until they
form a special bond and embark on an exciting but risky adventure.
ISBN 0–689–31682–8
[1. Grandfathers—Fiction. 2. Family life—Fiction.] I. Title.
PZ7.S84454Ed   1992
[Fic]—dc20   91–11922

Book design by Patrice Fodero

*For Mary and Bill
and Anne and Lawrence,
special people*

K.S.

Chapter 1

It was only the second of June, but already the class-rooms on the top floor of J. Harvey Wentworth Middle School felt like sweatboxes. Eddie Zitelli rubbed a trickle of perspiration from his upper lip and squinted at Mr. Chubman, striding back and forth in front of the sixth-grade social studies class.

"After Charles Martel stopped the advance of the Arabs"—Mr. Chubman whipped around to scrawl CHARLES MARTEL on the chalkboard in big, loopy let-ters—"he began a relationship with the pope that led to the start of the Holy Roman Empire."

Mr. Chubman jabbed the air with the stub of chalk for emphasis, and Eddie slid lower in his seat. How could Chub get so excited about a subject as boring as the Middle Ages?

Every kid in sixth grade called the social studies teacher "Chub," but only Eddie and Beanie knew how

1

appropriate that nickname was. "Listen to this!" Beanie had snickered, planting his finger on the dictionary page. "Chub: a freshwater fish." Perfect for tall, skinny Mr. Chubman, blinking like a goggled-eyed fish behind the lenses of his thick glasses.

Michelle Middleton, sitting in front of Eddie, swiveled to follow Mr. Chubman as though she were watching a close tennis match and didn't want to miss a stroke. What a phony. Eddie figured Michelle felt as much enthusiasm for the Middle Ages as she'd have for eating caterpillar sandwiches.

"In seven sixty-eight, Charles Martel's grandson Charlemagne became king of the Franks." Mr. Chubman's chalk dashed the name CHARLEMAGNE across the blackboard. King of the Franks. The first interesting thing Chub had said. Twelve minutes to lunch, and Eddie was starved.

His stomach rumbled, and Michelle flicked a glance over her shoulder. Eddie's stomach groaned a second time, and Michelle stifled a giggle. Then Eddie's stomach erupted like a whole bloody orchestra. Embarrassed, he waved his pencil in the air. Mr. Chubman nodded, and Eddie headed for the back of the room where the pencil sharpener was fastened to the wall beside the door.

Eddie turned the handle, tested the pencil point against his finger, and slid the pencil back in. He cranked the handle again, so hard that he broke the lead off. Pleased, Eddie began the whole process over.

Brrrring!!! The fire bell over the door clanged shrilly. "Remember, you guys go out exit three," Mr. Chubman called through the scrape of chairs.

Eddie tucked his pencil behind his ear and slid out the door. Whistling, he crossed the hall to the stairwell and trotted down the steps. At the bottom he halted, frowning. What idiot had placed two chairs in front of the doorway with a sign strung between them that said EXIT ON FIRE?

"Move it, Eddie!" complained the kid behind him, trampling Eddie's heels. Eddie pushed the chairs to one side and shouldered the door open.

As Eddie led the class up the sidewalk, Beanie scrambled alongside. "Good timing, huh? By the time the fire drill's over, it'll be lunch period."

"Hold it, you guys!" Mr. Malone, the gym teacher, came jogging across the grass, his silver whistle thumping against his chest. "You weren't supposed to come out that door."

"We were in social studies," Eddie explained. "Chub—Mr. Chubman's classes always use exit three."

"What's the problem?" asked Mr. Chubman, moving to the front of the crowd.

"Exit three was supposed to be blocked," snapped Mr. Malone. "Who moved the chairs?"

"Beats the heck out of me. Okay, you guys, who was first out?"

"It was you, wasn't it, Eddie?" piped Michelle.

Eddie scowled. That girl had a mouth as big as the

Mississippi. "I had to move those chairs," Eddie mumbled. "We couldn't get out with a rope across the doorway."

Mr. Malone's face reddened. "The doorway was blocked on purpose, Eddie! To see if you kids would have sense enough to find another exit."

"Guess you learned the answer to that one, Harry," said Mr. Chubman cheerfully.

"And now I'll have to explain it to Mr. Palmer. Eddie, if brains were eggs, yours would be scrambled." Mr. Malone strode off, shaking his head, and the classes began to file back into the building.

"Blocking an exit during a fire drill—I'll bet that's against the law," Eddie told Beanie indignantly.

"For sure. Hey . . ." Beanie tapped his wristwatch. "I was right. Lunchtime."

Eddie went to the cafeteria hoping he'd heard the last of the fire drill. But the following period, a student messenger appeared. "Eddie," said the science teacher, "you're wanted in the office."

He was in trouble for moving those chairs, Eddie felt sure of it.

On his way out Eddie passed the desk where Michelle sat, peeling flakes of purple polish from her thumbnail. Eddie wished he had a bottle of nail polish to pour over Michelle's head.

From behind the desk in his office, Mr. Palmer looked at Eddie. "Tell me, Eddie, what did you think that sign across the exit door meant?"

"I didn't." Eddie stuffed his hands into his pockets. "Think about it, I mean."

Mr. Palmer took off his glasses and rubbed the red spot on his nose. "That problem crops up often in your life, Eddie. I think it's time for me to have a talk with your parents. Stop by the office after school. Mrs. Holliday will have a letter ready for you to take home."

Eddie's stomach sank. An appointment with the principal . . . Mom and Dad would have a five-story fit.

He told Beanie about his problem on the way home. "If that stupid fire alarm had rung one minute sooner, I wouldn't have been at the pencil sharpener and some other kid would have found the blocked door."

"That was bad luck," Beanie agreed. "Pure and simple."

Beanie and Eddie split at the corner, and Eddie strode down Oak Avenue, scowling at the stiff white envelope that stuck out of his social studies book. Mom and Dad had enough problems right now with Pop in the hospital. They didn't need a summons to visit the principal. Once, just once, Eddie wished he could bring home the kind of letters his older brother, Tony, received, letters that said: Congratulations on making the honor roll . . . or being elected captain of the baseball team . . . or something else that impressed the heck out of everybody.

Eddie cut across the lawn and leaped the steps to the breezeway. Inside the kitchen, he dropped his social studies book on the table, took the pitcher of iced tea from the refrigerator, and lifted it to his mouth for a long, cold gulp.

"You've got the manners of a pig," said Tony, coming into the kitchen.

Eddie wiped his hand across his mouth. "Mom and Dad still at the hospital?"

"Yeah. Mom called a while ago. Said they'll be home soon."

Eddie peered at the sweatshirts and jeans piled in Tony's arms. "What are you doing with those clothes?"

"I'm moving downstairs. We're not sharing a bedroom anymore."

"What are you talking about? Tony!"

But Tony had vanished down the basement stairs.

Baffled, Eddie picked up his social studies book and headed through the dining room. He went up the hall to the bedroom he and Tony shared.

What the heck was going on?

Tony's rock posters had vanished from the walls. His baseball trophies were missing from the bookcase shelves. Behind the open closet door, only Eddie's shirts and slacks hung on the half-empty rod.

Tony brushed past Eddie. He opened his bottom bureau drawer and lifted out a pile of sweaters.

"What's the story, Tony?"

"I told you, I'm moving downstairs into Dad's office."

"Did Mom say you could?"

"Would I do this if she hadn't? Come on, Eddie,

you know we've asked Mom a hundred times to split us up."

Well, sure. He and Tony argued all the time. Tony said Eddie was a slob, Eddie complained about Tony's blaring stereo and weight bench. But he and Tony had shared this bedroom since their little sister, Mickey, was born eight years ago. Eddie had figured they were stuck living together until Tony went off to college.

"There's no shower in the basement," Eddie pointed out. "And no bureau for your clothes."

"I hung my suit and dress shirts in the cedar closet. Underwear and T-shirts I'll keep in cartons. And I don't mind walking up a flight of stairs to take a shower if I can escape from this junk." Tony jerked his thumb at the plane models crowding Eddie's bureau, the comic books slithering from under his bed, the layers of clothes that swathed the bedposts.

"I get this bedroom to myself?" Eddie demanded incredulously.

Tony's eyes, dark as ripe olives, slid away from Eddie's. "I said I'm leaving, didn't I?"

Tony strode out the door, singing: "Fly with me through purple nights, wild flights we'll share to-geth-e-er." Voltage, Tony's favorite group. Now Eddie wouldn't have to listen to Tony's crazy music anymore.

Eddie dropped his social studies book and flung himself across his bed. Hot dog! A bedroom of his own.

Eddie rolled onto his back. Overhead, in the center of the room, a row of smudges marked the ceiling.

Eddie winced, remembering Tony's reaction yesterday when he'd seen those marks: "You crummy cockroach! How'd you get your greasy pawprints on the ceiling?"

"It was an accident, Tony. I jump for the ceiling all the time," Eddie had explained. "But I've never touched before. If I'd known I could reach, I wouldn't have done it right after I fixed my bike chain, would I?"

Tony's eyes had raked Eddie from head to foot, as if Eddie were a stranger Tony had never seen before. "Stupid kid," Tony snarled. "Why am I stuck sharing a bedroom with you?"

Well, they didn't have to share a bedroom any longer. Down in the basement, Tony could pump iron, crank up his stereo, and plaster the walls with rock posters. And good luck to him!

Elated, Eddie surveyed his newly acquired space. He'd move over to Tony's bed, by the door, and dump clothes on his own. That way the floor and bedposts wouldn't always be a mess. He'd put his plane models on the shelf that had held Tony's trophies and stash his comic books and contest rules in Tony's bureau drawers.

Eddie went down on his knees beside the bed. Lifting the bedspread, he pulled out a shoe box holding the contest announcements he'd cut from cereal boxes, detergent cartons, and potato chip bags. ENTER THE LIVE-LIKE-A-MILLIONAIRE SWEEPSTAKES! blared the blue letters on the top piece of cardboard. Eddie studied the list of sweepstakes prizes longingly. He'd already sent nine entries to this contest. If he could scrounge up money for postage stamps, he'd send more.

"Tony sure cleared out fast," said Mickey from the doorway.

Eddie stared at the gray-striped cat in his little sister's arms, a yellow bow drooping from its tail, a doll's bonnet tied to its head. "For pete's sake, Mickey, what did you do to Jake?"

"Me and Jake are playing dress-up."

"You treat Jake like some kind of Barbie doll. Listen, Mickey, if somebody offered you five thousand dollars or a limousine to drive around in for six months, which would you take?"

"The money. I'd go to Disney World. When do you think Mom and Dad will get home?"

"Beats me." Eddie frowned at the list of prizes. Everybody visited Disney World, but how many kids got to ride in a silver limousine with a uniformed chauffeur at the wheel?

"Poor Jake," Mickey crooned. "Now you'll have to sleep in the basement."

"Jake can still sleep on Tony's bed. I don't care."

"No, he can't. He'd bother Pop."

Eddie stared at his sister. "What are you talking about?"

A car door slammed, and Mickey spilled Jake to the floor. "Mom and Dad are home."

"Hold it! What's this stuff about Jake and Pop?"

"Didn't Tony tell you? Mom phoned from the hospital. She said the doctor let Pop out early. Mom and Dad are bringing him here. Pop's going to sleep in this bedroom."

Pop was coming to stay at their house? That double-crossing Tony. He'd tricked Eddie big time.

Chapter 2

Eddie burst into the living room, fists clenched. "Liar!"

"I said I was moving out. I moved out, didn't I?" Tony retorted, opening the front door.

"You didn't say Pop was moving in!"

"Eddie, hush!" Mom struggled through the doorway carrying a tan suitcase, her eyes flashing a warning.

Behind her, Dad helped Eddie's grandfather over the threshold. A gnome of a man with wispy gray hair, Pop Zitelli leaned on a cane, his footsteps unsteady. Eddie was shocked at how frail his grandfather looked, shrunken and brittle as a dried leaf.

Then Pop saw Tony, and a familiar spark snapped in his eyes. "What do you think, Tony?" he wheezed. "That crazy hospital finally let me out."

Tony rocked forward to take the suitcase from his mother. "Hey, Pop, I'll bet you pinched so many nurses, they *threw* you out."

11

Mickey charged across the room and wrapped her arms around her grandfather. "Whoa!" said Dad. "Let Pop sit down, honey."

Dad eased Pop into an armchair, and Pop dropped the cane onto the floor. "Already I feel better, away from sick people."

"The therapy did wonders," said Mom, tucking a pillow behind Pop's shoulders. "But you still have a long way to go."

"How's a man gonna get well with all them nurses poking and prodding? Mr. Zitelli, here's your pill. . . . Mr. Zitelli, let me take your pulse. . . . Mr. Zitelli, have you had a bowel movement today? None of your business, I told them. Some things is private, even in the hospital."

Tony laughed. "I'll bet you told them good, Pop."

"You want to take a little nap before dinner?" asked Dad. "You're going to sleep with Eddie. Everything's arranged."

Eddie hunched his shoulders, recalling the mess in the bedroom. "I was going to tell you," Tony whispered. "They got home sooner than I figured."

Eddie edged toward the hall as Pop leaned back in the armchair, his brown eyes blurred behind his wire-framed glasses. "Okay if I stay here? I'll just close my eyes a couple of minutes."

"Anything you want, Pop. Anything at all."

Eddie headed for the bedroom and began pushing comic books under the bedspread.

"Eddie! You were supposed to have this room ready

for Pop." Exasperated, his mother set down the suitcase.

"I didn't even know Pop was coming," Eddie said indignantly. "Tony didn't tell me."

"Pop was supposed to spend another week in physical therapy—Dad and I figured we had plenty of time to discuss this with you boys. But we walked in to the hospital this afternoon and found Pop dressed to go home. He'd told the doctor he'd had enough. And you know Pop when his mind is made up—might as well argue with an avalanche."

"Why didn't you send me downstairs and let Tony stay with Pop?" Tony and Pop were buddies. Always had been. Everyone said Tony was the spitting image of Pop.

"Tony thought it would be better if he moved out because of his stereo and weight bench. Eddie, what's this?"

Uh-oh. Mom had picked up Eddie's social studies book. She was opening Mr. Palmer's letter.

Quickly Eddie explained about the blocked doorway. "Mr. Palmer didn't say I was in trouble. He just wants to talk to you."

"Principals don't invite parents in for social chats, Eddie." His mother read the letter, her forehead furrowing. "Tomorrow at three o'clock. Dad will be at work, and I don't want to leave Pop alone."

"Change the appointment," Eddie suggested. School ended in two weeks. Maybe Mom and Mr. Palmer would never get together.

With a sigh, his mother folded the letter. "No time is good right now. I'd better go tomorrow and get it over with. Pop can take a nap while I'm out. Bring me clean sheets from the linen closet, will you? And a pillowcase."

Eddie came back to find Tony's bed stripped. "Hey, I want to sleep in that bed."

Mom took the pile of linens from him and snapped a fresh sheet across the mattress. "Sorry, Eddie. I want Pop close to the door so I can look in on him during the night."

"Naps . . . bed checks . . . what is this stuff? You make Pop sound like an invalid."

"Your grandfather had a serious stroke."

"But he'll get better, won't he?" Eddie asked, alarmed. "It's not like when Mama Z was sick."

His mother's mouth softened. "Not like Mama Z, honey. But Pop needs our help. He can't do things for himself the way he used to."

Eddie watched Mom empty the contents of Pop's suitcase into the bureau. Rats. All his plans to store comic books and contest rules in those drawers, down the drain.

"For heaven's sake, look at these." Mom held up several packets of crackers she'd taken from the bottom of the suitcase. "The hospital must have served these on Pop's dinner tray."

"Why would he save a bunch of stupid crackers?"

"Pop and Mama Z lived through the Great Depression, Eddie. They didn't believe in throwing anything away." Mom closed the suitcase. "Put this in the attic for me, will you? I'm too tired to walk another flight of stairs."

That night Mom served dinner in the dining room. A welcome-home celebration for Pop, Eddie figured—until he realized that six people wouldn't fit around the kitchen table.

Dad cut Pop's lamb chop into little pieces. Pop ate a few bites, then laid down his fork. "A little more," Mom urged. "You have to eat to get your strength back."

"I had enough," said Pop.

"What about some applesauce? Try a spoonful of applesauce."

"The dinner's very good, Diane. But I don't want no more."

"A few weeks from now, Pop will be scraping the flowers off his plate," Dad said, his voice hearty. "You'll see. Corky Zitelli, he's an eater."

"Don't forget your pills." Mom tipped over the paper cup she'd set at Pop's place. Two pills rolled out, one yellow, one brown.

"Bunch of nonsense, all this medicine," Pop muttered.

"The pills are important, Pop. For your blood pressure and your heart."

"Diane's right," said Dad. "That medicine is going to make a new man of you."

"Eighty-three years I been happy with the old one," said Pop. He edged his chair back, his mouth pinching into an obstinate line. "I'll take them in the bathroom. I don't need no help," he added as Dad stood up. "I ain't no invalid."

"I'm headed for the living room. We can walk together, can't we?"

Mickey and Tony left the table next while Eddie was eating a second helping of chocolate pudding, so Eddie got stuck helping with the dishes. First trip out to the kitchen, Mom scolded him: "I've told you not to stack dirty dishes. Look, Eddie, you got mashed potatoes all over the bottom of these plates."

Next trip Eddie carried two glasses, one in each hand.

"Eddie, if you're trying to make me angry, you're about to succeed beyond your wildest dreams. Use a tray and do the job right. I've had a hard day, and I have more to do tonight than wash dishes."

Hey, thought Eddie, me too. He planned to work on his Tiger Shark plane model, in case anybody cared.

When Mom finally turned him loose, Eddie headed for the bedroom. He pulled up short at the doorway. Dad straddled a straight chair beside Tony's bed with Pop facing him. Pop's head was tucked between his shoulders. "Bunch of baloney!" Pop snorted.

"Come on, Pop. You have to do what the doctor says."

"In the hospital maybe. Not outside the hospital."

Dad's jaw muscle tightened, and he shot Eddie a glance that said scram. Jeez. Pushed out of his own bedroom!

Eddie stumped into the bathroom and stared into the mirror over the basin. A cowlick poked from the crown of his head. Eddie wet his fingers and slicked the hair down. As soon as he let go, the cowlick sprang up again.

Eddie had light brown hair, same as Mom and Mickey. But Mom's hair curled on the ends. So did Mickey's. Eddie's hair was stiff and straight. Tony took after the Zitelli side of the family—thick, shiny black hair and olive skin. Tony had Dad's even teeth too. Eddie rubbed his tongue across his wire retainer. Lucky Tony.

Eddie tilted his head toward the door, listening to Pop and Dad. They were speaking Italian now, Dad's words coming slow and clumsy, Pop shooting back rapid bursts. Bored, Eddie opened the medicine cabinet. He took out Dad's shaving cream, shook the can, and squirted his name in foam across the vanity: Eddie Zitelli. Not bad. Maybe he'd be a skywriter when he grew up. Eddie shook the can again, ready to write another message.

"Out!" said Dad from the doorway. "Pop needs the bathroom."

Eddie edged past Dad and Pop. Whew. He hoped no one ever had to help *him* to the bathroom. He grabbed the box holding his plane model from the closet shelf and carried it into the dining room.

Eddie was sorting pieces of the Tiger Shark on the dining room table when Mom tapped him on the shoulder. "Why aren't you doing homework?"

17

"School's practically over. Teachers don't give homework anymore."

"Then why did you bring home your social studies book?"

"Chub said to read the last chapter. But that's not homework. Homework is stuff you have to hand in."

"The teacher's name is Mr. Chubman, Eddie. And read the chapter before you work on your model."

Oh, boy. Back to the bedroom again. Dad was helping Pop put on a pair of striped pajamas. Eddie took his social studies book to the dining room table and flung himself into the chair.

Soon Dad leaned on the table beside him. "Pop's asleep. Don't turn on the light when you go into the bedroom."

"How am I supposed to get undressed?"

"In the dark. Like it's no big deal. This has been a rough day, Eddie. Your mother and I need a little co-operation."

How come he was always asked to cooperate? Eddie wondered. Why didn't anybody ever offer to cooperate with him?

Actually the bedroom wasn't that dark. Mom had told Eddie to leave the door ajar so she could check on Pop during the night, and the lamp in the hall cast a yellow glow through the crack. Still, it was too much trouble to hunt for pajamas, so Eddie went to bed in his underwear.

Mom and Dad turned in early too. Eddie heard the toilet flush. Then the bedroom door closed. Silence.

Eddie lay on his back, his hands laced beneath his head. Tony should be sleeping here, across from Pop. Tony, Pop's buddy. When Eddie and Tony were little, before Mickey was born, Eddie's family used to drive over from New Jersey to Philadelphia every Sunday to have dinner at Pop and Mama Z's house. Aunt Tess and Uncle Leo came too, with their kids Lisa and Joey. And Father Charles, until he was sent to work in Brazil. Tony always sat next to Pop, and Pop would feed him bits of buttered bread and pieces of fruit Pop dipped into his wine glass. When Mom protested, Pop just waved his hand: "What wine, Diane? A few drops is all he got."

Eddie rolled onto his side. What the heck was that weird noise, sort of a slow wheeze ending in a rattle? He threw back the sheet and padded across the room. Bending close to Pop's bed, Eddie heard Pop draw a shallow breath. When Pop exhaled, his dentures clicked like dice rattling in a cup.

Eddie stalked back to bed. How was he was supposed to fall asleep listening to that racket? He wondered if Pop had always breathed that way. Maybe it had something to do with the stroke.

Eddie remembered the Saturday Pop took ill. They were in the kitchen eating lunch, and Tony had just told a funny story. When the phone rang, Dad tipped back in his chair to reach it. As he listened to the caller, the laughter drained from his eyes.

"That was Joe," he told Mom. "Pop's in the hospital. He was giving Sam Casale a haircut, and he just fell down on the floor. Like someone hit him with a hammer, Joe said."

Eddie figured that hitting Pop with a hammer was about the only way to get him into a hospital. Pop never had thought much of doctors, and after Mama Z died Pop said doctors were no good. No *damn* good. But, then, Pop didn't like depending on anyone. Mom might be right that Pop needed help, but lots of luck convincing Pop of that fact.

The bedroom door nudged open, and a shadow glided across the floor. "Jake," Eddie whispered. "Over here."

Ignoring Eddie, Jake leaped onto Pop's bed. Pop didn't stir. Hey, if Pop didn't feel the cat curled against him, what difference? It just proved that it was the bed Jake liked, not Tony.

And right now, Eddie wasn't real fond of Tony either.

Chapter 3

In Eddie's dream, the mail carrier was handing him an envelope that said Special Delivery. Eagerly, Eddie ripped the envelope open and read the letter inside: "Congratulations! You have won first prize—"

The words fell apart as someone shook Eddie's arm. "Eddie, wake up."

"I'm awake," Eddie murmured.

"Don't disturb Pop," whispered his mother.

"Right . . ."

Eddie blinked sleepily. Across the room, Pop lay on his back, lips puffing in and out. Jake had vanished. Mom must have carried him off when she checked on Pop during the night.

Eddie shut his eyes, trying to recover the dream. *Congratulations! You have won first prize. . . .* He hadn't even noticed which contest it was, and he'd entered dozens.

"Eddie!" A second, no-nonsense whisper came from the doorway.

Eddie rolled to the side of the bed and sat up. He yanked on the jeans and T-shirt he'd left in a heap on the floor, then remembered that he hadn't changed his underwear. Too bad. He'd put on clean socks to make up for it.

Gym class today. Eddie rummaged in the closet to find his gym bag. When he unzipped the top, a rank odor shot up his nostrils. Phew! Eddie spilled out gym shorts, a pair of wrinkled socks, and a damp towel rolled around high-top sneakers. That's what stank—his sneakers. He'd have to dry them out or kids would need gas masks when he walked into gym class.

Eddie carried the sneakers into the bathroom. Tony stood in front of the mirror, blow-drying his hair. Eddie braced the sneakers between his legs and the cabinet door and spread toothpaste on his toothbrush.

"How'd Pop sleep?" Tony asked.

"Lying down."

"An eleven-year-old comedian. Or is eleven your IQ? Hey, what stinks?"

"Beats me."

"Smells like old clam shells. You better find out what that smell is and do something about it, or they'll run you out of school on a rail."

Tony put the hair dryer into the bathroom closet and left, whistling. Eddie took the hair dryer out, plugged it in, and set to work on his sneakers.

"Eddieee!" Mickey's head poked through the door. "Mom says come to breakfast *now*."

Eddie touched his sneakers. Dry enough. He grabbed Mom's can of scented bath powder and dusted the insides of the sneakers for good measure.

Mom was toasting frozen waffles when Eddie slid in at the breakfast table. She handed Eddie a glass of orange juice and spoke to Dad. "What time will you be home, Don?"

"Around six-thirty."

"Can't you make it earlier? In the hospital, Pop ate dinner at five o'clock."

"Sales meeting at four. No way we'll be finished before five. Then I have phone calls to make. Can't you feed Pop early?"

"And serve dinner twice? I have enough to do, thanks. I have to fit in that meeting with Mr. Palmer this afternoon too."

The orange juice turned sour on Eddie's tongue. He'd forgotten that appointment. Mom was right. Principals didn't meet with parents just to shoot the breeze. One way or another, Eddie faced trouble today.

"Let Pop wait and eat with us. A couple of hours difference in mealtime won't kill him."

His mother frowned and handed Eddie his waffle. "Eat. You're late."

As he picked up the maple syrup, Eddie noticed a dark shadow at the bottom of the bottle. He held the bottle up to the light. Shoot. The shadow came from his fingers.

"Eddie, you don't have time to fool around," his mother scolded.

"I thought I saw a mouse in the maple syrup bottle," Eddie explained, pouring a trail of syrup across his waffle.

Tony grimaced. "What would a mouse be doing in the maple syrup?"

"I read this article. In the newspaper," Eddie explained as he ate. "Some lady found a dead mouse in a bottle of maple syrup. The company paid her ten thousand dollars because the syrup made her sick."

"She ate maple syrup that had a mouse in it?"

"I guess she didn't notice the mouse when she used it."

"Gross!"

Eddie shrugged. "I'd eat syrup with a dead mouse in it for ten thousand dollars." At least he thought he would. Eddie put another piece of waffle in his mouth. He chewed slowly, wondering what mouse-flavored syrup tasted like.

"Eddie, stop dawdling and finish your breakfast."

Abruptly, Eddie pushed back his plate. "That's all I want."

"Don't forget your retainer. I'll see you in Mr. Palmer's office at three o'clock." Mom shot him a stern glance. "And stay out of trouble, okay?"

Eddie folded his hands together. "I'll wear wings and a halo all day."

Beanie was waiting for him on the corner. "Guess what I brought in my backpack."

"A jar of grasshoppers," Eddie said with a grin.

"No grasshoppers! Never again."

Two weeks earlier, Eddie and Beanie had caught grasshoppers in the field behind Beanie's house to feed the white rat in science class. On the way to science, Beanie handed the jar to Eddie. Somehow it dropped. Broken glass and grasshoppers flew everywhere. The custodian wasn't amused.

"This is something for gym class," Beanie went on.

Eddie rubbed his hand across Beanie's backpack. "A Frisbee! Hot dog! I hope Mr. Malone lets us use it. Sure would beat playing softball." Eddie stunk at softball, dribbling out easy grounders when he batted, dropping fly balls when he was in the out-field.

But Eddie had to get through social studies before worrying about gym class. Most teachers had stopped new work and started to review. Not Mr. Chubman. "We'll end the year with oral reports on the Middle Ages," Chub announced.

Everyone groaned, Eddie loudest of all. Who wanted to do a crummy oral report the last two weeks of school? And Eddie couldn't afford a poor grade. His average was exactly seventy. One failing grade would suck him down the drain.

Mr. Chubman rubbed his hands together like a used-car salesman about to move a lemon off the lot. "I want you to find out about everyday life in the Middle Ages—food, clothing, transportation, kinds of buildings, dif-ferent classes of people."

Mr. Chubman began to assign topics, and Eddie slid

lower in his seat. Maybe Chub would run out of ideas before he reached Eddie.

A fly buzzed through the open classroom window. Eddie leaned sideways, raising a cupped hand.

"Eddie, are you listening? Write your topic down."

Eddie jerked his hand back. "Sure, Mr. Chubman. Right away."

What had Chub said? Something about pheasants. Eddie wrote *pheasants* in large letters and underlined it twice. Weird topic. What was special about pheasants in the Middle Ages? Maybe people ate them at banquets or something.

Heading down the hall after social studies, Eddie nudged Beanie. "You got the Frisbee?"

Beanie slapped his backpack. "Right here."

But Mr. Malone was absent, and the sub shook his head. "Plan book says softball, you play softball." The sub was a college jock with rippling muscles and a T-shirt that looked sprayed on.

Ken Cook nudged Eddie. "Ain't that something? A talking plan book."

"For subs who can't read," Eddie muttered.

In the first inning, Eddie dropped a fly ball. Second inning, he struck out. Softball stunk.

Back in the locker room, Beanie spun the Frisbee on his finger. Eddie beckoned, and Beanie flipped the Frisbee to him. "Watch it," Ken warned. "I'll bet that sub eats Frisbees for dinner."

Beanie glanced over his shoulder. "He won't see us. He's back in Malone's office reading the plan book."

"Reading?" Eddie scoffed. "You mean looking at the pictures." He flung the Frisbee to Ken. Too low. Ken lunged and winged it back. The Frisbee flew over Eddie's head, struck a heat pipe, and dropped onto a radiator grille suspended from the ceiling.

The boys stared up at the radiator. "Can't reach the Frisbee from here," said Eddie. "Maybe from the top of the lockers."

Beanie shook his head. "Forget it. If the sub catches you scrambling around on the lockers, he'll ship you straight to the office."

That prospect stomped through Eddie's stomach in football cleats. But Eddie was taller than Beanie or Ken, so he'd have the best shot at reaching the radiator. Besides, it was his fault the Frisbee had landed up there.

"What's the sub doing?"

"Still has his nose stuck in the plan book."

"Give me a boost."

Beanie groaned. "Make it fast," he urged, linking hands with Ken.

Eddie hoisted himself onto the top of the locker and stood up, wiping dusty palms against his shorts. The radiator was at chest height, and farther out than he'd thought.

Up and down the aisle, kids were watching him while they changed out of gym clothes. Balancing at the edge of the locker, Eddie reached toward the radiator. The metal grille teased him, just inches from his fingertips.

Eddie stretched farther and felt his heels rise from the locker. He jerked back violently, prickles of alarm racing along his spine. He couldn't reach the radiator that way. Only one thing to do. Eddie took a deep breath and fell forward across open space. His fingertips landed on the edge of the grille.

"You got it!" Ken said beneath him.

Not quite. Eddie was balanced precariously, his hands just touching the grille, most of his weight still on his feet. The Frisbee lay in the middle of the radiator, eight inches away. To reach it, Eddie would have to lean farther out, shifting more weight onto his hands. If he slipped off the locker, he'd hit the concrete floor and probably break his neck. If he tore the radiator loose, Mr. Palmer would break his neck for him.

Eddie licked his dry lips and eased forward, keeping a wary eye on the metal straps that attached the radiator to the ceiling. Nothing groaned, nothing popped. Heart thudding, Eddie braced himself on one hand and worked the other hand across the radiator grille toward the Frisbee.

"Eddie—" Beanie's pale face stared up. "The sub's leaving the office!"

Eddie snatched the Frisbee and shoved himself backward. In one quick movement, he fell to his knees and sprawled on the gritty metal.

"Okay, you guys. Let's see a little hustle."

The sub was headed up their aisle! Eddie pressed his cheek to the top of the locker. He felt as conspicuous as King Kong clinging to the Empire State Building. If the sub glanced up and saw him, King Kong was a dead duck.

Chapter 4

"How come you two haven't changed yet?"

Ice formed in Eddie's veins. The sub was talking to Beanie and Ken!

"Crank it up, guys. Bell rings in two minutes."

The sub strode on through the maze of kids and disappeared around the corner. At once, Eddie swung over the side of the locker and dropped to the floor. He held the Frisbee out to Beanie.

"You did it!" A grin split Beanie's face.

Ken rolled his eyes. "When Mr. Muscles stopped to talk, I figured you were a goner."

Eddie peeled off his gym shorts and reached for his slacks, heart hammering. "Nothing to it," he croaked, success as sweet on his tongue as cotton candy.

But leaving the locker room, Eddie remembered where he was headed next and his elation melted.

"Mr. Palmer's expecting you," said Mrs. Holliday,

the school secretary. Her eyebrows rose. "Eddie, you look as if you fell out of a cement mixer. Tuck in your shirt and smooth down your hair."

Eddie jammed his shirt inside his jeans and ran his hand over his cowlick. Then he knocked at the door to Mr. Palmer's office.

Mom was seated in a chair opposite the desk. Eddie slid onto the second chair.

"I've been telling your mother about the fire drill, Eddie," said Mr. Palmer. "I know you meant well when you opened that blocked exit, but you didn't use your head. That's Eddie's biggest problem, Mrs. Zitelli—he seldom uses his head. Last week Mr. Malone asked Eddie to move the volleyball net. Eddie dragged the stand instead of lifting it and left a three-foot scratch in the gym floor. The week before that, Eddie filled the fish tank in science class and forgot to remove the hose from the tank. All the water siphoned out. That was hard on the fish as well as the floor." Mr. Palmer took off his glasses, polished the lenses, and put them back on. "I feel sure Eddie can do better if he puts his mind to it."

How? Eddie wondered miserably. He certainly didn't set out to cause these problems.

"I understand, Mr. Palmer. We'll work on Eddie's sense of responsibility," Mom promised.

"Good," said Mr. Palmer. And the meeting ended.

As they left the building, Mom slid on her sunglasses. She led the way across the parking lot without a word. Inside the car, Eddie braced for the explosion.

"That was an impressive list of disasters Mr. Palmer recited. He's right, Eddie. You don't—" Mom broke off. She lifted her sunglasses, frowning. "What's that smudge on your face?"

Eddie rubbed his cheek and looked at his fingertips. "Dirt. From the top of the gym lockers."

His mother took a deep breath. "I'll bite. How did dirt from the top of the gym lockers wind up on your face?"

As Eddie explained, his mother's head slipped to one side. "Let me get this straight. While I was waiting for Mr. Palmer to tell me you lack common sense, you were scaling a gym locker to recover a Frisbee? Eddie, you are impossible!" She glanced at her watch and her mouth puffed with exasperation. "Almost four o'clock, and I still have to stop at the supermarket. We'll finish this discussion later."

Relieved, Eddie rolled down the window and let cool air rush past his face. He'd escaped Mom's wrath, at least for now.

At the supermarket, Eddie pushed the cart through the produce section while his mother picked up an eggplant, broccoli, and two bags of carrots. Eddie wrinkled his nose. "How come all these vegetables?"

"I want to be sure Pop eats nutritious meals."

Eddie shook his head. His notions of good nutrition leaned heavily toward combinations of pizza and potato chips.

They turned up the cereal aisle, and Eddie's eyes roved the shelves, searching for contest announcements. Bingo! A row of yellow cereal boxes trumpeted: WIN THE COCOA CRUNCHIES CASH-IN. As Mom went on ahead, Eddie tipped a cereal carton off the shelf and read the contest rules printed on the back: "Compare the picture below with the card inside the carton. If the pictures match, you're an instant winner."

An instant win—just what Eddie needed. A dose of good luck to chase away the bad, like aspirin driving off a headache.

The picture on the cereal carton showed a red-haired boy seated at a kitchen table eating a bowl of Cocoa Crunchies. A yellow clock hung on the kitchen wall, and a striped cat lay curled at the boy's feet. The caption beneath the picture read: TIME FOR THE WORLD'S BEST BREAKFAST.

Eddie studied the gray-striped cat. A dead ringer for Jake. Maybe that cat was an omen. Maybe Eddie was meant to win this contest.

Eddie hurried after his mother. "Can I buy this cereal?"

His mother glanced at the carton. "Sugar-coated? Not on your life."

"Please, Mom," Eddie begged. "Just this once. If the pictures match, I'll be an instant winner."

Mom looked at Eddie through narrowed eyes. "If I let you buy the cereal, will you eat vegetables every night for a week without complaining?"

"It's a deal!"

"Whoa." Mom caught his wrist. "The last time you opened a box of cereal to take out contest rules, you didn't close the top and the cereal spilled all over the checkout counter. Wait till we get home."

Impatience seethed in Eddie's chest as he trundled the cart behind his mother while she finished her shopping. An instant win! If only the pictures matched.

When they pulled up the driveway, Mom said, "I'm going inside to make sure Pop's okay. Carry in the groceries before you open that cereal box, Eddie."

Eddie lifted the car trunk and scowled at the three sacks of groceries. He hoisted one paper bag in his left arm, the second in his right. Shoot, he could manage the third sack too. Bracing one bag on his hip, Eddie picked up the remaining bag by the top. No problem. He'd come back later to close the trunk.

As he climbed the breezeway steps, Eddie could practically hear the picture card ticking inside the cereal carton, ready to set off an explosion of dollar bills. He set down the extra bag of groceries and opened the storm door. Propping the door with his foot, Eddie picked up the bag. He kicked the door wide and stepped forward. The spring rebounded, and the door whacked Eddie from behind, knocking him into the kitchen.

The paper sack in his hand ripped loose, and groceries spilled to the floor. The eggplant landed with a thud, oranges scattered like billiard balls, and a carton of eggs spun against the table leg. Uh-oh. Eddie set the other bags on the counter. Gingerly he picked up the egg carton. Three eggs were cracked, two smashed.

"You dropped my groceries!" groaned his mother from the doorway. "Eddie, you are impossible!"

33

"I'll pay for the broken eggs," Eddie promised. "Honest. And if I win the contest, I'll buy you a whole flock of chickens."

"Just what I need—a dozen Rhode Island Reds scratching around the backyard." His mother threw up her hands. "For goodness' sake, end the suspense. Take a look inside that cereal box."

Eddie dug through the groceries for the carton of Cocoa Crunchies. He pried the flap open and drew out the picture card. Eagerly he compared the two pictures. The captions matched. So did the red-haired boys. Two bowls. Two spoons. Two striped cats.

The screen door banged open. "Coach ended baseball practice early," said Tony. "Mom, you left the car trunk open."

The pictures were identical! Eddie turned the card over and read the message on the back: IF THE PICTURES MATCH, YOU HAVE WON $500.

"I'm rich!" Eddie gulped.

Chapter 5

Eddie pushed the picture card and cereal carton at Tony. "The pictures match. I won five hundred dollars!"

Tony studied the contest rules and shook his head. "Earth to Eddie, earth to Eddie. What time is it, peanut brain?"

"Quarter of five. Why?"

"Not on our clock, dimwit. Here, in these pictures."

Eddie snatched back the box and picture card. His mother peered over his shoulder. "That's a shame, honey. One clock says eight-thirty, the other says eight-thirty-five."

"Yeah, Eddie, when the big hand is on the six—"

"They wouldn't count something as small as that, would they?" Eddie protested.

"The directions say match, not come close. Tough toenails, Eddie."

"I was robbed!" Eddie collapsed onto a chair.

"You missed out on five hundred dollars, I lost my flock of Rhode Island Reds," said Mom. "Bad luck for both of us. How about setting the dining room table to take your mind off your disappointment? You put away the centerpiece, and I'll get out the glasses and silverware."

Eddie slouched into the dining room burning with indignation. Of all the rotten unfair contests! He'd write a letter to the Cocoa Crunchies people complaining about those picky rules. And for sure he'd never buy their stupid cereal again.

Eddie lifted the bowl of silk flowers off the table and set it on the buffet beside the day's mail. Hey, maybe he'd heard from some other contest. Eddie shuffled through the mail. Nothing for Eddie Zitelli. But a tan envelope addressed to his father bore a tantalizing message: DONALD ZITELLI MAY WIN A MILLION DOLLARS.

"You can open any contest offers I receive," Dad had told Eddie, "and you can have any prizes I win." So far Dad hadn't won a thing. Still, somebody had to win these contests or they wouldn't be legal, right?

Eddie headed for the bedroom, slitting the tan envelope as he went. "Pop, how you doing?"

Pop, just up from a nap, sat on the edge of the rumpled bed in his stocking feet, his gray hair a fuzzy halo over his ears, his sleeveless undershirt hanging from his narrow shoulders. "I'm doing fine, Eddie. If I was doing any better, it'd be against the law."

Eddie unfolded the letter. A line of dark print

36

shrieked from the top of the first page: SEND IN SWEEP-STAKES CARD—FIRST PRIZE ONE MILLION DOLLARS! Eddie turned to the second page and found what he expected: a block of stamps offering reduced rates on magazine subscriptions.

Eddie scowled at the stamps. These sweepstakes offers always said: "No purchase necessary to enter." But people who sent money for subscriptions had to have an edge over people who didn't. Eddie felt sure of it. Rats. How could he subscribe to a magazine when he couldn't even afford postage stamps?

"Eddie, you were supposed to set the table!"

Eddie thumped his fist against his forehead. "I forgot, Mom. Honest. I'll do it now."

"Between the kitchen and the dining room, you forgot you were supposed to set the table? No wonder Mr. Palmer thinks you're rowing with one oar out of the water."

"I stopped to look at the mail—"

"And found a contest offer, right?" His mother shook her head. "I'll set the table myself. You help Pop get ready for dinner."

"What help? I don't need no help."

"Eddie can lace your shoes so you don't have to bend over."

Mom vanished, and Pop scratched his head. "Naps. People tying my shoelaces. I ain't used to this stuff. Eddie, don't worry about me. Go on and do whatever you want to do."

Eddie watched as Pop bent down to tie the laces on

his black shoes. When Pop sat up again, he was wheezing and red blotches stained his cheeks. He pushed himself to his feet and picked up the green plaid sports shirt on the end of the bed. Pop stroked the shirt, the stubborn lines melting from his face. "Mama Z gave me this shirt. Pretty classy, huh, Eddie?"

"Yeah, Pop, real sharp." Eddie figured it was the wrong size though. The collar gaped around Pop's thin neck, and the shoulder seams drooped.

Pop limped toward the door. "Let's go, Eddie. The boss won't like it if we're late for dinner."

Dinner was tuna-and-noodle casserole, broccoli, and a tossed salad. Broccoli. Yuck. And he'd promised to eat vegetables without complaining. Eddie poked at the tuna casserole. "Second time today I've eaten fish. School cafeteria served Deep-Sea Dandy for lunch. What's dandy about fried fish on a roll?"

"Eddie, pass me the salt," said Pop.

Mom snagged the salt shaker before Eddie got his hand on it. "Dr. Kilkenny said you should cut down on salt."

"All my life I been using salt on my food, all my life I been healthy. I don't see no reason to stop now."

"Salt's bad for your blood pressure, Pop. Dr. Kilkenny explained that." Pop's jaw poked out stubbornly, and Mom let go of the salt shaker. "Okay. Okay. A little salt won't hurt, but take it easy, will you?"

"Mom, is it all right if Joe comes over tonight? He's got the new Voltage album."

Eddie figured Tony was just trying to distract Mom

so she wouldn't notice that Pop was shaking salt on his food like crazy. Mom never minded when Joe came over, but Eddie couldn't stand him. Half a head taller than Tony and built like a bull, Joe was a varsity wrestler. He loved to show how strong he was by putting a headlock on Eddie.

"I'm going to the library after dinner," Eddie announced. "To work on my social studies report."

"Pop, you want Eddie to bring you a book? A detective novel maybe?"

"I don't need no books. TV's enough for me."

"Can I have money for the copy machine?" Eddie asked.

"Take a couple of quarters from the change jar." Mom was still watching Pop. "Don't forget to take your pills, Pop."

"You told me about the pills last night, Diane. I'm not one of the kids, you got to tell me the same thing every day." Pop lurched to his feet.

"You're not finished, are you? You hardly touched your dinner."

"I ate all I want." Pop shook the contents of the paper cup into his hand and shuffled from the room.

Eddie saw his mother's exasperated face. Better get out before Mom roped him into the dishes again. Eddie excused himself from the table, grabbed three quarters from the change jar in the kitchen, and headed out the door.

The evening was mild, the air filled with the smell of freshly mowed grass. Eddie walked over to Center

Street and turned toward the library. Half a dozen kids from his social studies class were in the library working on their reports, but luckily for Eddie no one was using the *P* volume of the encyclopedia.

The encyclopedia wasn't much help. The entry under Pheasants said that pheasants were game birds. Males had brilliant plumage and long tails, and hens were brown. Great. Unless he could find more information, Eddie would be presenting the shortest oral report in the history of J. Harvey Wentworth Middle School.

The card catalog listed four books on birds. The first book included a whole page on ring-necked pheasants. Pleased, Eddie fingered the three quarters in his pocket. He could photocopy this page for twenty cents—or buy a bottle of soda at the Quickie-Shop for sixty cents.

Easy decision. Eddie borrowed a pencil and paper at the circulation desk and copied down the information on pheasants. Then he folded the sheet of notes into his pants pocket and left the library.

At the Quickie-Shop, Eddie took a bottle of soda from the refrigerator case and headed for the cash register. A lanky boy with brown hair stood ahead of him in line, also buying a bottle of soda. "Yo, Eddie," the boy greeted him. "What's happening?"

"Nothing much," said Eddie, pleased that Tug had spoken to him. An eighth grader, Tug Buckley was famous at J. Harvey Wentworth Middle School for taking eleven years to reach eighth grade, much of that time spent sitting on the bench outside Mr. Palmer's office.

Outside the store, Tug turned in the same direction as Eddie. They crossed the street and started down a block lined with houses. Tug unscrewed the top from his soda and took a deep swallow. "I heard the custodian busting on you and that skinny kid—what's his name, Beanie?—last week in the hall. What happened?"

"We had a jar of grasshoppers," Eddie explained sheepishly. "Jar broke. Grasshoppers took off."

"No kidding. Guess you gave the custodian a four-star fit." Tug drained his soda and wiped his arm across his mouth. "Eddie, my man, you are a cool dude." He flipped the empty bottle into the base of a hedge along a nearby vacant lot.

A cool dude. Swaggering a little, Eddie finished his own soda and pitched the bottle after Tug's. But the angle was wrong. Instead of thudding into the dirt, the bottle vanished through a gap in the hedge. Eddie heard a sharp crack.

"Uh-oh," said Tug. "Sounds like trouble."

Chapter 6

Tug spun around and sprinted up the street, away from the brown-shingled house on the far side of the hedge. Eddie raced after him, his stomach churning. More rotten luck. He never tossed soda bottles into vacant lots—Mom and Dad were dead set against littering. But when Tug pitched his bottle into the hedge, it had seemed like the cool thing to do.

They rounded the corner, and Tug slowed to a walk. "You've got a wild right arm, Eddie."

"What do you think I hit?"

"Beats me. Don't sweat it—nobody saw us. Stay loose, Eddie."

Eddie watched while Tug cut across a yard and hopped a fence. Should he go back to that brown house to find out if he'd broken something? He didn't dare. Eddie needed another problem like a swing seat needed splinters.

The streetlights were on and crickets were shrilling by the time Eddie circled back to Oak Avenue. As he mounted the breezeway steps, Eddie heard the whang of electric guitars through the basement window. Voltage. Joe was still here.

Behind the screen door, he saw his parents seated at the kitchen table. "We can't ask Tess to help," Dad said as Eddie reached for the door. "She has enough to handle."

"That's not my point—" Mom broke off, seeing Eddie. She matched a pair of socks from the pile in front of her and rolled them into a fist. "Did you finish your report, Eddie?"

"I have the information. All I need to do is write it up." Running had made him thirsty. Eddie opened the refrigerator.

"You want something?" Dad asked.

"I'm thirsty."

"Get a glass of iced tea and keep moving. Your mother and I are talking."

Pardon me for living, thought Eddie. He filled a glass with tea and added ice cubes. As he started out, his mother leaned across the table, a flush reddening her cheeks. "He fights me every step of the way, Don."

She meant Pop. Mom wanted Pop to follow the doctor's orders, while Pop was determined to do things his own way.

Pop and Mickey were playing checkers in the living room. "Who's winning?" Eddie asked.

Pop winked. "You think I got a chance against the checker champion of New Jersey?"

Eddie ambled back to the bedroom, sipping his tea. He could write up the notes he'd made at the library, but he'd wasted enough of Friday night on school work. Instead Eddie set his glass on the bureau and shucked off his sneakers and socks. Sitting cross-legged on the floor, he took out the shoe box of contest announcements and spread the contents around him.

Eddie eyed the scraps of paper and pasteboard hungrily. "Win the car of your choice. . . . Two weeks in Hawaii. . . . You may already be a winner. . . ." TV sets, bicycles, fur coats—the possibilities were endless. He was bound to win a prize if he kept entering. Eddie felt sure of it.

He picked up the rules to the Live-Like-a-Millionaire Sweepstakes. Deadline was next week. He had time to send more entries, if he only had stamps. Eddie scowled, remembering the money he'd wasted on that stupid bottle of soda.

Mom had told him not to take her postage stamps, but maybe she wouldn't mind if he just borrowed one. He'd return it as soon as he got some money.

Headed for his parents' bedroom, Eddie heard Dad's voice from the living room, then Pop's, quick and gruff. Sounded like Dad was preaching the gospel according to Dr. Kilkenny, and Pop wasn't buying it.

His parents' bedroom was crowded. A card table stood against one wall with cartons of papers lined up beside it. Dad must have moved stuff up from his office.

Eddie squeezed around to Mom's side of the bed. Mom kept her writing paper and stamps in the night table drawer. As he rummaged through the drawer, Eddie saw the notepad on top of the night table, containing a list in Mom's neat handwriting:

Medicare—make copies of bills
Appt. with Dr. Kilkenny
Prescription refills
Pop's house—taxes and water bill

"Eddie, stay out of my stamps!"

"I only wanted to borrow one. One measly stamp."

"No stamps. Out!" His mother picked up her hairbrush and brushed her hair with quick, hard strokes.

Eddie slunk from the room. What had put Mom in such a prickly mood?

Eddie stepped into his bedroom and found Pop standing just inside the doorway, staring down at the contest rules. "Already my legs don't work so good," Pop growled. "You want to clean this stuff up before I fall on my ear?"

Without a word, Eddie shuffled up the contest rules and dumped them into the shoe box. Dad had kicked him out of the kitchen. Mom had scolded him for taking her stamps. Now Pop was complaining because Eddie had scattered a few pieces of paper on the floor. The whole world was against him.

Pop was unbuttoning his shirt. "You getting ready for bed, Pop?"

"You think I'm going out dancing?"

Now Eddie was being pushed from his own bedroom. Indignantly he slid the shoe box under the bed and turned toward the door.

"Listen, Eddie, don't leave on my account. You can keep the light on. It don't bother me."

"That's okay, Pop," Eddie mumbled. "I'm headed out to the kitchen anyway." He paused, watching Pop fold his shirt and lay it on the bed. Pop bent down to untie his shoes, his lumpy fingers fumbling at the knots.

"Hey, Pop, let me do that." Eddie slipped off Pop's shoes and socks. Pop's feet were cold, the pale skin webbed with veins.

"Hell of a thing, a man can't take off his shoes without gettin' dizzy," Pop muttered. "Thanks, Eddie. You put them shoes under the chair."

"Right."

Balancing the empty glass on his hand, Eddie strode up the hall. The door to his parents' bedroom was closed. So was Mickey's. In the living room, Dad sat before the TV, his face shadowed.

Tony, dressed only in shorts, was at the kitchen table eating pretzels. Perspiration gleamed on his chest and shoulders. Eddie poured himself more iced tea and flung himself into a chair across from Tony.

"You been lifting?"

"No, genius, I always sweat like this. Hey, how was the conference with Mr. Palmer?"

47

"Okay."

"Meaning he talked about the weather? He asked Mom's opinion on the Phillies?"

Eddie shrugged. "He told Mom I can do better in school. That I don't use my head."

Tony rolled his eyes. "Words of wisdom. You've got to shape up, Eddie. You're going into seventh grade next year, and you still wander through life like a turkey stumbling up to the chopping block."

Eddie took a long swallow of iced tea. He needed a change in luck, not a sermon from Tony. "Tony, does Aunt Tess have a problem?"

"What are you talking about?"

"I heard Dad say something to Mom."

"Beats me. At Aunt Tess's age, I guess being pregnant's problem enough. How old's Lisa—a year older than me? And Joey's thirteen. Now Aunt Tess is going to have a baby. That's a big gap between kids."

Eddie took another sip of iced tea, thinking. "How long do you figure Pop will stay here?"

Tony shrugged. "If it was up to Pop, he'd go home tomorrow."

How come it wasn't up to Pop? Didn't he have anything to say about his own life? Eddie reached for the pretzels and knocked over his glass of iced tea. "Hey!" Tony barked, shoving his chair back.

"Jeez . . . I'm sorry, Tony." Eddie grabbed the dishrag and mopped the tea. "I'm really sorry."

"You dumb baboon. I'm soaked!"

Eddie choked back laughter. The tea had run into

Tony's lap, staining the front of his shorts. Tony looked like a little kid who'd peed in his pants.

Tony pushed Eddie against the refrigerator, his eyes hard. "What are you laughing at?"

"Nothing. I'm not laughing."

"You better not be," Tony snarled and stalked out of the kitchen.

While Eddie was wiping up the floor, the phone rang. "Is this Eddie the nerd?"

"What do you want, Joe?" Cradling the receiver on his shoulder, Eddie wrung the dishrag over the sink.

"Where's your manners, kid? Let me talk to Tony."

"Tony's in the shower."

"Tell him to call me as soon as he gets out."

"You were just here half an hour ago. Didn't you two talk enough? Or maybe you need Tony to read you a bedtime story."

"You want a fat lip, Eddie? Just do like I told you."

Eddie scowled and hung up the phone.

The shower was running as Eddie rapped on the bathroom door. "Yo, Tony."

"What do you want?"

Eddie opened the door so he wouldn't have to shout.

"I asked what you wanted, I didn't invite you in," Tony snapped from behind the shower curtain.

"You don't own the bathroom." Eddie stepped inside to prove it. "Just because you're taking a shower doesn't mean I can't use the toilet."

"Flush that toilet now, and you're dead!"

Eddie had once flushed the toilet while Tony was

showering, not realizing that the toilet would draw off all the cold water. He'd almost scalded Tony. But it was an accident, Eddie thought indignantly. Tony should know he'd never do it again. Instead, Eddie wrenched the hot water handle on the basin. Hard.

The shower curtain billowed, and Tony let out an icy howl. "You toad!"

"Just washing my hands," Eddie sang out and ducked from the bathroom.

Pop was asleep, but he'd left the lamp lighted. Eddie closed the bedroom door, kicked off his sneakers, turned out the light, and dived into bed.

Seconds later, footsteps thumped across the hall. The door opened, and Eddie heard Tony's hard, angry breathing. Finally the door clicked shut. In the darkness, Eddie grinned. For once, he'd outfoxed Tony.

When Eddie woke the next morning, Pop's bed was empty. Butter-colored sunlight filled the room, and a blue jay squawked outside the window.

Eddie walked barefoot to the kitchen. Dad and Pop were eating cereal. Tony was reading the sports page of the local newspaper.

"Where's Mom?"

"Took Mickey to the eye doctor."

"What's for breakfast?"

Dad flipped his hand at the cereal cartons and bananas on the kitchen counter.

"Can I make french toast?"

"If you clean up when you're finished."

Eddie opened the refrigerator in search of eggs. "Something's sticky," he said, lifting one bare foot.

Tony glowered at him over the newspaper, and Eddie ducked his head. He'd forgotten about the spilled iced tea. "How did you sleep, Pop?"

"Who can sleep with crickets hollering all night and birds making a racket the minute the sun comes up?"

"Better than the hospital though, right, Pop?" said Dad.

"Hospital was a loony bin. All night people walking up and down the halls, nurses leaning over you to make sure you're not dead."

"Even crickets are better than that," Dad pointed out.

"My own house is better yet. On Del Monte Street, a person wants quiet, he's got quiet. When I'm back home, I'll sleep like a baby."

Dad stood up, poured two mugs of coffee, and set one in front of Pop. "Pop, I been thinking. That physical therapy you were getting in the hospital. It helped a lot. You don't want to lose the strength you built up. You ought to exercise, take a walk every day."

"Where am I gonna walk?"

"Around the neighborhood. Chat with the neighbors."

Pop's eyes narrowed. "This is Diane's hot idea. Why do I want to walk around here? I don't know none of your neighbors. Home on Del Monte Street, I'll walk. In the city I got places to visit, people to talk to."

The phone rang, and Tony leaned back to grab it. "Yeah, Eddie's here." He held out the receiver.

"Eddie?" It was Tug. "The guy who lives in the brown house just called. Some lady saw us running down the street and gave him my name." Eddie held his breath, waiting for the punch line. "No hard feelings, Eddie, but I'm not taking the rap for something I didn't do. You gotta go see this Mr. Peck. Right away."

Chapter 7

Pedaling toward the brown-shingled house, Eddie searched for damage the soda bottle might have caused—a chipped shingle or a dented downspout. Nothing. Eddie leaned his bike against a tree, his spirits taking a cautious upturn. Maybe the guy who lived here just wanted to scold him for throwing trash into his yard.

Eddie rang the doorbell, and footsteps rustled inside. A narrow-faced man with gray hair opened the screen door. "Yes?"

"I—uh—came about the soda bottle."

"You're the boy who broke my storm door!" Mr. Peck's face tightened into a scowl. He came out onto the porch and clapped a hand on Eddie's arm. "Come with me, young man."

He marched Eddie around the corner of the house. Eddie's bottle lay unbroken on the rubber mat below the side door. A jagged crack sliced across the glass panel in the top of the door.

"I left that soda bottle right where it landed," Mr. Peck told Eddie.

Eddie's stomach squeezed into a knot. "I didn't mean to break your door," he apologized. "I was aiming for the hedge."

Mr. Peck's long nose quivered indignantly. "That vacant lot is not a dump, young man. Don't you know better than to throw your trash on other people's property?"

Mr. Peck fished a slip of paper from his shirt pocket and waved it sternly at Eddie. "I called the hardware store. It will cost eighteen dollars and sixty-five cents to have that glass replaced. I'm taking the panel to the store today, and it will be ready Wednesday. You bring me the money Tuesday evening, or I'll call the police and let them handle this problem. Now, come into the house so I can write down your name and address."

The police . . . Eddie's knees sagged. This wasn't ordinary bad luck, it was a major disaster. Mom and Dad would go up in flames if they knew Eddie had broken somebody's storm door. But without their help, where would he find $18.65?

When Eddie dragged through the kitchen door, Tony was loading the dishwasher. "Where did you run off to? You were supposed to clean up the breakfast dishes." Tony shut the dishwasher door and reached for the phone. "Dad said to empty the wastebaskets."

Tony had money stashed away, Eddie thought as

he pulled a plastic trash bag from the box on the shelf in the utility room. If Eddie explained the jam he was in, maybe Tony would help him out.

When they were kids, Tony had bailed Eddie out of trouble more than once. Like that long-ago Sunday afternoon at Mama Z and Pop's when Eddie, age seven, had sneaked into the barbershop at the front of the house. Eddie loved Pop's barbershop—the shiny chairs that cranked up and down, the bottles of sweet-smelling hair oil and shaving lotion, the drawers filled with rubber combs and barber shears. He'd taken a pair of shears from a drawer, the metal cold and slippery in his hand. Standing on tiptoe in front of the mirror, Eddie had lifted a lock of hair and snipped it off. Then another lock. *Snick . . . snick.* Bits of hair drifted to the floor.

"Eddie! Mom's going to kill you." Tony's eyes, round with horror, stared into the mirror over Eddie's shoulder. Looking at his ragged reflection, Eddie realized suddenly what he'd done and began to blubber.

"Don't cry," Tony told him. "Give me those scissors." Tony evened out the worst spots. Then he let Mom believe he'd been playing barber with Eddie, so he shared the scolding.

Eddie felt a bubble of hope rise through his swamp of gloom. Tony wouldn't let Mr. Peck hand him over to the police. Tony would come up with the money.

He turned back to the kitchen. Tony was leaning on the counter, talking on the phone. "I'd have loved to go with them, Mrs. Cairo. What time did Joe call?"

Joe's phone call! He'd forgotten to mention it to Tony. Tony would chop him into hamburger. Eddie darted out of the kitchen and headed for his bedroom.

Dad and Pop were having another talk. Dad jerked around to look at Eddie. "What do you want?"

Eddie waved the plastic bag. "I'm emptying wastebaskets."

"Eddie!" Tony pushed him from behind. "Joe's mom says he called last night. Wanted me to go to today's Mets game in New York with him and his dad. When I didn't call back, his dad invited their next-door neighbor instead."

"I meant to tell you about the phone call. That's why I came to the bathroom. But I forgot."

"You *forgot*? Frog-brain! I ought to—"

"Hey, argue somewhere else," Dad ordered. "Pop and I are busy."

In the hall Eddie faced Tony. "That's the truth, Tony. I forgot. I'm sorry."

"You ought to be sorry," Tony snarled. "For living!"

Tony stomped off, and Eddie slumped against the wall. He could hear the gates of doom clang shut. There was no chance Tony would lend him money now.

Eddie drifted from room to room dumping wastebaskets and hunting desperately for a solution. Maybe he could get a job. Sure, and maybe Superman would fly in to save him. He had to find someone to lend him the money. It was his only hope.

When Mickey and Mom arrived home, Eddie cornered his sister in her bedroom. "Mickey, you got any money?"

Behind her new glasses, Mickey blinked like a baby owl. "What for?"

"I broke something. And I have to pay for it."

"What did you break?"

"Never mind. Can you lend me money or can't you?"

"Okay. For ten do-whatever-I-say's."

"Robbery!" But Eddie was desperate. "All right, all right. How much money do you have?"

Mickey took a lumpy knee sock from her bureau drawer and shook a shower of change onto the bed. "Almost three dollars."

Three dollars? Eddie's hopes collapsed. "Forget it. I'll rob a bank or something."

Eddie went out to the backyard and sat at the picnic table, his shoulders hunched. He should get a rope and hang himself right now, get the whole thing over with.

Wait a minute. There was one more person he could try. Beanie.

In Beanie's family, finances went up and down. Mr. Beane made good money as a house painter, but he took long breaks between jobs.

Mr. Beane had once explained his work schedule to Eddie. He was sitting on the front porch at the time, feet propped on the railing, a glass of lemonade in his hand and a book on his lap. "Life is short, Eddie. A man has to save time for the things that matter. The family. Books. A little gardening."

57

When Mr. Beane wasn't working, the Beane family often went camping in the Pocono Mountains or down at the New Jersey shore. As soon as the money ran out, Mr. Beane went back to work. Right before Mr. Beane started working again, when money was running low, Beanie brought weird lunches to school. On Monday, Eddie would take a look at Beanie's lunch. That would tell him whether Beanie was likely to have extra money.

In the cafeteria on Monday, Eddie watched Beanie empty out the contents of his brown paper bag. An overripe banana, a jar of cold baked beans, and a single graham cracker. Eddie's hopes melted like butter in the microwave. "Looks like your dad's been out of work for a while," he said gloomily.

Beanie nodded. "Mom's digging deep for meals. We had pea soup and sardines for dinner last night. What's up, Eddie? You look like a corpse they forgot to bury."

"I'm in trouble, Beanie. Big trouble. I broke some guy's storm door, and I need eighteen dollars and sixty-five cents to pay for it."

Beanie whistled. "How did that happen?"

Eddie told him the story. "Where are you going to get the money?" Beanie asked.

"Beats me."

Beanie picked up his banana, then put it down again. "Hey, I can help you out. Dad gave me twenty bucks for my birthday back in March. I hid the money in a mug on the fireplace mantel and forgot about it till just now. I'll bring that twenty bucks to school tomorrow."

Eddie felt as though he'd been snatched from the

edge of a crumbling cliff. "Beanie, you saved my life. I'll pay you back as soon as I can."

"No hurry." Beanie grinned. "I feel like my twenty bucks just worked a miracle—I brought a corpse back from the dead!"

Eddie's good mood lasted until social studies class. "Tomorrow we start oral reports," said Mr. Chubman. "Remember, you need a written copy of your report to hand in to me."

Eddie chewed his thumbnail. He'd remembered the written copy but forgotten the oral part. With the information from the library, he felt sure he could write a decent report. But what if the class fell asleep during his oral presentation? He needed a visual aid, something that would grab kids' attention.

Beanie stayed after school for newspaper club, so Eddie headed home alone. At Center Street, he turned toward the town's business section, searching store windows for inspiration

The display window in the hardware store featured camping equipment: propane stoves, flashlights, hatchets. Maybe he could take in a hatchet and explain that people used hatchets back in the Middle Ages to chop off pheasants' heads. Nah. Dumb idea.

The bakery window held crusty loaves of bread and trays of sugared doughnuts. Eddie imagined waving a loaf of bread in the air—"Pheasants eat bread crumbs." That idea was worse than the hatchet.

The next display window held weird stuff—a leather trunk draped with a shawl, a tray of costume jewelry,

59

a dusty painting of an Indian riding a spotted pony, dented candlesticks, several china teapots, a row of unmatched cups and saucers. Eddie glanced at the black lettering across the top of the window: SARAH'S SECOND-HAND TREASURES. Looks more like leftovers from a garage sale, Eddie thought.

His eyes wandered back to the Indian. Maybe Sarah would have a painting of a pheasant. Eddie pushed open the door and stepped inside.

A woman with crinkly brown hair sat at the counter working a crossword puzzle. "Can I help you?" she asked. Eddie figured she was Sarah.

"I wondered if you had a painting of a pheasant."

"A pheasant?" Sarah cocked her head, her silver earrings swinging.

"I'm giving an oral report on pheasants. In school. I figured a picture would make things more interesting."

Sarah tucked her pencil behind her ear. "Good thinking. Most oral reports are a drag. Unfortunately, I don't have any pheasant paintings at the moment."

Shoot. "Thanks anyway," said Eddie.

"Hold on a minute," Sarah said as he turned toward the door. "I have something else you might be able to use."

Chapter 8

Sarah led Eddie through a curtained doorway into a back room jammed with furniture, bric-a-brac, and stacks of books. She squeezed past a curio cabinet and picked up a carton. "How about a real pheasant to go with your report?"

The stuffed bird Sarah lifted from the carton had a bronze breast and coppery black-spotted sides. A ring of white feathers circled its neck, and tufts of green feathers, like horns, stood up on top of its head. Above the bird's yellow beak glowed a pair of red glass eyes.

"Awesome!" Eddie breathed. "How much?"

Sara wiggled the pheasant's cracked tail feathers. "Poor bird's been through hard times. You can have him for six dollars."

Six dollars. After Eddie paid for the storm panel with Beanie's twenty dollars, he'd only have $1.35 left. Eddie felt as though the world's greatest Christmas gift had been snatched from his fingers. Then inspiration struck. "I can't afford to buy the bird. Could I rent it for a day?"

Laugh wrinkles fanned from Sarah's green eyes. "I don't usually rent merchandise, but I guess I could make an exception. How much do you think I should charge?"

"How about a dollar thirty-five?" Eddie asked hopefully. "I don't have the money now, but I can pay you when I return the pheasant."

"What's your name?"

"Eddie Zitelli."

Sarah slid out the pencil tucked behind her ear. "You drive a tough bargain, Eddie Zitelli. Let me write down your name and address so we can make this transaction official."

Eddie carried the carton home as tenderly as if he were transporting eggs for his mother. Suddenly life looked brighter. Thanks to Beanie's loan, he could pay Mr. Peck and jazz up his social studies report too.

Eddie stopped, thunderstruck. Maybe this was the stroke of good luck he'd been hoping for. Maybe Beanie's offer of twenty bucks had broken the string of disasters afflicting his life.

Mom was in the kitchen, scraping carrots at the sink. "You're late, Eddie. You weren't kept after school, were you?"

"I walked over to Center Street. Guess what I brought home." Eddie slid the carton onto the kitchen table.

"That box had better not contain a hamster, a bird,

or any other creature that needs to be fed and kept clean."

"Bird? Did you say bird? Mom, you have X-ray vision." Triumphantly Eddie lifted the pheasant from its carton.

"What's that mangy thing?" Tony asked from the doorway.

"A pheasant."

"Looks like a feather duster that was attacked by killer moths," scoffed Tony. "Where did you find it?"

Eddie explained about Sarah and her secondhand treasures. His mother put down the carrot scraper. "Come show it to Pop. Tony, you come too."

In the living room, Eddie set the pheasant on the coffee table. Pop's bristly eyebrows pulled together. "What do you got there?"

"A stuffed pheasant. It's a visual aid to go with my social studies report."

"What does a pheasant have to do with social studies?" asked Tony.

"Beats me. Mr. Chubman gave out dumb topics to fill up the last week of school."

"I thought maybe your mother was gonna roast that bird for dinner," Pop teased.

"Speaking of dinner," Mom put in quickly, "we have a half hour before we eat. Tony, why don't you and Pop take a little walk? Help Pop work up an appetite."

"I don't want no walk," said Pop.

Tony shook his head, edging toward the door.

"Can't do it. Coach said we had to complete two hundred sit-ups before baseball practice tonight. I haven't started."

Mom turned to Eddie. "Then you go with Pop."

"I have to write my social studies report," Eddie protested.

"You can write the report after dinner."

Pop's lower lip rolled out mulishly. "I said I don't want no walk."

"You need the exercise."

"I told you, Diane, when I get home, I'll exercise."

"That may not be for a while. Eddie, help Pop up."

Mom wasn't about to give in. The blotchy veins in Pop's pear-shaped nose darkened. Ignoring Eddie's hand, he worked himself up from the chair and limped toward the front door.

Mom flew to the coat closet and took out Pop's cane. "Make him use this, Eddie," she whispered. "He's not steady on his feet."

Eddie scowled, wondering how he'd gotten snagged instead of Tony. Reluctantly he followed Pop out onto the stoop. Pop lurched down the first step, and Eddie grabbed his arm. "Mom said to use your cane."

Pop's cheeks puffed, and he grunted something in Italian. Ignoring the cane, he thudded unsteadily down the remaining steps and jerked along the front walk.

Eddie looked at the cane. If Pop didn't want it, he sure wasn't going to haul it around. He propped the cane against the maple tree and dashed after Pop.

Pop was clumping along the sidewalk, his face

pinched and stubborn. "You're doing good, Pop," Eddie said cheerfully. "How far you want to go?" Pop didn't answer. Mom had really gotten Pop's goat this time.

Pop limped as far as the next driveway, then turned unsteadily. As they started back, Eddie saw Beanie skid up the driveway on his bike. Good old Beanie. He'd brought the twenty bucks over so that Eddie could stop worrying.

Beanie knocked on the breezeway door, and Mom opened it. Eddie heard her say, "Hi, Beanie." Then her gaze moved past Beanie to Pop and Eddie. "Back so soon?" she called. "How was your walk?"

Pop said nothing. He hauled himself up the front steps and vanished through the living-room door. As Eddie crossed the lawn to the breezeway, he saw the flush that colored his mother's face.

Mom turned back into the kitchen, and Eddie flung himself into a chair on the breezeway. "How's it going, Beanie?"

"Not so hot. I found this note in the mug on the mantel."

Warily Eddie took the note Beanie handed him. As he read it, he felt himself slide back toward the edge of that crumbling cliff. "IOU $20. Will return money as soon as Dad gets paid. Mom."

The cliff gave way under his feet, and Eddie plunged through the air with the hard ground rushing up to meet him.

Chapter 9

"Can you wait till Friday?" asked Beanie, his face screwed up with concern. "My dad started work today. He gets paid Friday."

Eddie shook his head. "I'll think of something. Don't worry about it."

"I feel awful about this, Eddie."

"I'm telling you, it's okay."

Beanie rose, shuffling his feet. "Well, see you tomorrow."

Yeah. If Eddie didn't throw himself under a freight train during the night. Now he had Sarah to worry about, as well as Mr. Peck. Looking ahead, Eddie could see only disaster.

At dinner, Eddie ate little, his appetite crushed by the weight of his gloom.

"Don, pass Pop the mustard. Put a little mustard on your ham, Pop. You'll like it that way."

"Listen to the thunder. It's going to rain."

"I don't want no mustard."

"No kidding, Mickey Mouse. I thought thunder meant a snowstorm was coming."

"Tony, don't call me Mickey Mouse!"

Eddie pushed his plate away. "May I be excused?"

"Before we have dessert? I made brownies."

"I'm not hungry, Mom."

"I don't want no dessert either," said Pop.

"A dish of frozen yogurt?"

"No thanks. I don't want nothing."

"Don't forget your pills."

"I got them, Diane. They're right here in my hand."

Eddie hurried back to the bedroom and flung himself across the bed, burying his head in his arms. Nothing had changed. Bad luck was still beating him black-and-blue.

He heard Pop's slow shuffle, then a bureau drawer scraped open. Eddie sneaked a look at Pop, standing by the bureau with his black leather change purse in his hand. Would Pop lend him twenty dollars? Pop closed the purse and dropped it into the drawer.

Eddie wasn't sure Pop even had twenty bucks he could spare. Grandmother Mayes, Mom's mother, sent Tony, Eddie, and Mickey twenty dollars every birthday and Christmas. But Grandmother Mayes lived in a fancy apartment with a doorman at the front door. She had closets filled with silky dresses and blue-waved hair that always looked as though she'd just left the beauty parlor. Pop and Mama Z owned a narrow row house in South Philadelphia. Mama Z had worn cotton dresses with an old sweater buttoned over them and coiled her gray hair into a bun on the back of her head.

Besides, Pop and Mama Z had a lot of people to give presents to: Eddie's family; Aunt Tess, Uncle Sal, and their two kids; and Father Charles. The families Father Charles worked among in Brazil were so poor they lived in packing crates. Mom and Dad sent money to Father Charles every month. Maybe Pop did too. Add in bills for doctors and medicine when Mama Z was sick, and it wasn't likely Pop had any extra cash. But Eddie was desperate. He had no place left to turn.

"Pop . . ."

"What?"

"Can I ask you something?"

"You got a mouth, don't you?"

Pop sounded cranky as a bear stuck in a barrel. "Never mind," Eddie muttered.

"What do you mean, never mind? You got something to say, say it."

"I wanted to ask a favor."

"So ask it."

Eddie took a quick breath. "I'm in trouble, Pop. I broke this man's storm door, and I need twenty bucks to pay for it."

"What are you telling me, Eddie? How did you break a storm door?"

"It was an accident. I threw an empty soda bottle

into a vacant lot. At least, that's what I meant to do. The bottle went through the hedge and cracked the glass in this guy's door."

Pop plucked at his lower lip. "Things you do in life, you got to take responsibility for them. That's what it means to be a man. But not to have money when you need it, that's hard."

Pop took his change purse from the drawer and opened it. He drew out a twenty-dollar bill, and a yellow pill dropped to the floor. Eddie handed the pill to Pop and took the money Pop held out. "You're saving my life," Eddie said with a sigh of relief.

Pop grinned, his dark eyes dancing. "To save a life takes more than twenty dollars. I'm saving only your skin—the piece stretched over your backside."

"I owe you, Pop."

Eddie strode out the door and headed for his bike. No sense waiting till tomorrow. He'd ride over to Mr. Peck's house with the money right now.

When Mr. Peck saw Eddie on his porch, his face turned stern. "You'd better not be here to make excuses, young man. That money's due tomorrow."

Eddie held up the twenty-dollar bill.

Mr. Peck dug into his pants pocket and counted out Eddie's change. "I hope this will teach you not to throw trash into other people's yards," he said in a testy voice.

I only did it once, Eddie thought defensively. Breaking the storm door was an accident. But Pop's words echoed in his head: *Things you do in life, you got to take responsibility for them. That's what it means to be a man.*

All right, what he'd done was a little bit stupid. A lot stupid. But at least he'd paid Mr. Peck, and it was over with.

Pedaling home, Eddie felt a gust of wind and the first fat drops of rain from the approaching thunderstorm. He swerved up the drive, then skidded to a stop by the maple tree. Pop's cane! Right where Eddie had left it. Thank goodness he'd seen it there. Mom would have been furious if that cane sat out in the rain.

Inside, Mom was rushing from room to room, closing windows. Eddie rounded up paper and a pen, ready to begin his social studies report. He set the pheasant in the middle of the dining room table for inspiration.

The bird was dynamite, no question about it. Michelle had once dressed as the Statue of Liberty to give a report on immigration, but Eddie's pheasant would be even more impressive. Tony was right though. The tail feathers looked a little scraggly, and the bird was dusty. After he wrote the report, he'd clean up the pheasant and tape its tail back together.

Now Eddie needed the notes he'd taken in the library. The notes were in his pants pocket. The pants should have been hanging on his bedpost. But the bedpost was empty. Eddie hurried into the bathroom and flung back the lid on the clothes hamper. The hamper was empty too.

Eddie burst into the kitchen. "Mom, have you seen my brown pants?"

"I just put them in the washer, along with a bunch of other clothes you left lying around your room."

Eddie sank onto a kitchen chair, horrified. "The notes for my report were in those pants!"

Mom clapped her hand to her mouth. Then she grinned. "You think you have a dummy for a mother? I always check the pockets of your pants before I do laundry. Your notes are right there, on the shelf beside the sink."

Eddie grabbed the piece of paper. "You're wonderful, Mom. I promise I'll hang up my clothes every day from now on."

"Sure. And pigs will fly. Go do your report, Eddie."

Writing the report was harder than he had expected. After fifteen minutes of scribbling and scratching out, Eddie still hadn't found a good opening. Maybe he should take a break. Clean up the pheasant, then get back to the report.

Eddie dusted the bird and wiped off its claws and beak. But when he tried to straighten up the pheasant's tail feathers, the feathers broke off in his hand. Eddie hunted up a roll of cellophane tape and carefully taped the feathers back on. Then he tried again to begin his report.

Maybe it would help if he gave the bird a name, something that sounded like the Middle Ages. Frederick for instance. Frederick the Pheasant. That was a little too fancy. Eddie shortened it to Fred the Pheasant. Yeah. Suddenly Eddie's imagination kicked into high gear. Across the top of the page, Eddie printed: "A

Day in the Life of Fred the Pheasant." Then he began to write.

Next morning, Eddie met Beanie at their usual corner. "Pop loaned me twenty dollars," Eddie announced.

The worried expression melted from Beanie's face. "Your grandfather's all right. I was afraid I'd be visiting you at the county jail. What's in the carton?"

"Beanie, you'll never believe it. Wait till you see the visual aid I found for my social studies report. Mr. Chubman's going to give me an *A* for sure."

"What is it?"

"Wait and be surprised, Beanie. I guarantee this visual aid will knock your socks off."

When Eddie walked into social studies, he went straight to Mr. Chubman. "Can I make my report today, Mr. Chubman? I brought a visual aid to go with it."

"Always glad to see a little creativity!" said Mr. Chubman, his eyes crinkling behind his thick glasses. "You can go first, Eddie."

Eddie strode to the front of the room and set the carton on Mr. Chubman's desk. The class watched curiously as Eddie took out his written report and cleared his throat. "My report is entitled 'A Day in the Life of Fred the Pheasant.' "

He sneaked a quick look at the class. Mr. Chubman was leaning forward, a puzzled expression on his face. Maybe he couldn't hear, Eddie thought. Eddie cleared his throat a second time and read louder.

"One summer morning back in the Middle Ages,

the king of the Franks called his knights together. 'I'm giving a banquet tomorrow,' Charlemagne said. 'I want you to catch a pheasant so the cook can roast it for my guests.' The knights took their bows and arrows and set out for the forest. Meanwhile, in a clump of bushes deep in the forest, Fred the Pheasant was just waking up."

Eddie laid down the report and reached into the carton. Dramatically, he lifted Fred into the air. Kids craned their necks for a better view, and whispers buzzed through the room. No doubt about it, they were impressed. Pleased, Eddie continued: "Pheasants are handsome birds. The males have brown feathers, and—"

"Hold it." Mr. Chubman unfolded his long legs from the student desk where he was sitting. "Is this a joke? You were supposed to talk about *peasants*, Eddie. People—not birds."

Peasants? Stunned, Eddie stared at Mr. Chubman.

Michelle let out a giggle, and Eddie thumped Fred down on the desk. The cellophane tape broke loose, and Fred's tail feathers fell off. Gusts of laughter rolled through the classroom. Even Beanie's face turned crimson, his cheeks puffing as he tried not to laugh.

Mr. Chubman rapped on the desk, glowering at Eddie. "Put that ridiculous bird on the bookcase with your report. Then sit down. And see me after school this afternoon."

Eddie slunk back to his desk, his face burning. Peasants, he thought. Not pheasants. People, you dummy, not birds. He'd just made the stupidest mistake in the history of the world.

Eddie's disaster accompanied him to the cafeteria. Ned Duffield tapped Eddie on the shoulder in the lunch line. "That pheasant of yours was a real turkey."

"There was fowl play in Chub's class," cackled Iggie Madison. He tucked his hands into his armpits and flapped his elbows. "Cluuuck, cluuck, cluuck!"

"Aw, why don't you go pound sand," Eddie protested feebly. He grabbed his lunch tray and slunk to a table in the rear of the cafeteria.

Beanie joined him there. "Too bad, Eddie. That visual aid sure cooked your goose—" He broke off, grimacing. "Sorry. I didn't mean to say that."

Eddie shook his head slowly. "I can't believe it. I just get Mr. Peck off my back and this happens! Beanie, my life couldn't be worse."

"Not true, Eddie. Go home with an *F* in social studies—"

Eddie finished for him. "And my life will get worse."

Mr. Chubman was waiting for Eddie after school. He held up Eddie's report, his face stern. "I want the truth, Eddie. Were you doing this to be funny?"

"Mr Chubman," Eddie said, his voice heavy with misery, "I rented that bird to make my report more interesting. Would I spend money on a joke?"

Mr. Chubman leafed through the report. "It's obvious that you did research. Actually, your report is very interesting—I especially liked the part where Fred led the knights into the swamp. But didn't it occur to you that a report on pheasants was a little off center for social studies?"

"I figured you just gave out crazy topics to keep us busy till school ended," Eddie admitted. He jammed his hands into his pockets. "Problems like this keep happening to me, Mr. Chubman. I think I'm jinxed."

"Clean the cotton out of your ears, and you'll eliminate a lot of your bad luck, Eddie," Mr. Chubman said dryly. He opened his grade book and ran his finger down the page. "You know what happens if you get a zero for this assignment?"

"I flunk social studies. Then I find a bridge and jump off."

Mr. Chubman's mouth flicked into a smile. "I don't want to be responsible for your untimely death, Eddie. I can see that you worked hard on this report, and I believe you honestly misunderstood the assignment. So I'll leave your average where it is. Exactly seventy."

He'd been snatched from the jaws of death! "Thanks, Mr. Chubman," Eddie sighed.

"Consider it a tribute to your creativity." Mr. Chubman's eyebrows twitched. "I've heard of pheasant under glass, but you're the first student who ever served me pheasant in class."

"Mr. Chubman," Eddie said with dignity, "if that was supposed to be a joke, you just laid an egg."

Chapter 10

Eddie maneuvered through the last week of school like a soldier stepping across a mine field. He came home the final day relieved that he had survived sixth grade. Summer was bound to be easier, right?

Not right.

Mom had stopped insisting that Pop carry his cane, but she was still pushing for afternoon walks. Eddie could see Mom's point. Pop spent so much time in that brown armchair in front of the TV it was lucky he hadn't taken root in the upholstery. He limped worse now than when he left the hospital. But Mom's coaxing only made Pop more stubborn. If she'd lay off, maybe Pop would make up his own mind to exercise.

Or maybe not. Pop was stubborn, but Eddie figured something else was involved. Pop was like a runner resting up before a race. He'd exercise when he returned to Del Monte Street, Pop said. But whenever

77

Pop talked about going home, Mom and Dad changed the subject.

Meanwhile, Mom had begun a tug-of-war with Pop, and Eddie was caught in the middle. Every afternoon Mom said, "Eddie, why don't you take Pop for a walk?" Like Pop was a pet poodle, and Eddie could snap on a leash and lead him up the block.

At first Eddie had protested. "Why can't Tony walk with Pop?"

"Tony's busy."

Yeah, digging shrubs at a nursery during the day and lifting weights at night. So busy he never stopped by the bedroom to chat with Pop. Tony had always been athletic, but lately he'd turned into a muscle freak. He'd even put up a chinning bar. Eddie learned about it one evening when he went to the basement in search of a screwdriver. Tony was standing against the doorway to the cedar closet, a book balanced on his head, a pencil in his hand. "Practicing to be a model?" Eddie teased, mincing down the steps.

Tony pulled the book off his head, color surging into his face. "I'm measuring for a chinning bar if it's any of your business. Which it's not."

So Tony earned money and built muscles while Eddie was stuck taking Pop for walks. And that was as easy as moving an elephant out of a mud hole.

Mom would suggest a walk. Pop would refuse. Mom would insist, and Pop would hunker down in his chair. But Mom always kept prodding until finally Pop would haul himself to his feet, his cheeks an angry purple.

Outside Pop shuffled along, stiff as a puppet with overtight strings, his mouth flattened into an obstinate line. Pop would go halfway up the block, then turn and stump back.

The first day Eddie struggled to make conversation, but Pop barely responded. Second day, same thing. After that, Eddie stopped trying and they walked in silence.

Then, about two weeks into the summer, a squirrel darted across the sidewalk. Eddie swung up an imaginary rifle. "Pow!" The squirrel whisked under a hedge and vanished.

"You missed," Pop grunted.

Surprised, Eddie said, "I'll nail him next time."

"You own a BB gun?"

"I wish. Mom won't let me."

End of that conversation. But the next day, Eddie tried again. "Hey, Pop, did you own a BB gun when you were a kid?"

Pop shuffled a few steps before he replied, as though he was hunting through his memory for the answer. "Back in Brooklyn when I was ten, I had a friend named Mario owned a BB gun. I fell in love with that gun. Wanted one so bad I could taste it."

Eddie tried to imagine Pop at ten, a year younger than Eddie was now. "Did you ever get a BB gun, Pop?"

"Those days, there wasn't no money in my family for toys. My father, he paved streets six days a week. Came home tired, covered with mud. But right before

Christmas, my father took a second job on Sundays, working for a man made venetian blinds. And Christmas morning, I find this long box under the tree."

"Your gun?"

Pop nodded. Eddie waited, hoping to hear more.

"After church, I go over to Mario's house to show off my gun. Mario's mother is visiting next door, and Mario wants to impress me he's a better shot than I am. He points at the Christmas tree and says, 'You see that red ball?' Bang!"

"Did he hit the ball?"

Pop gave a rusty chuckle. "Not the red one—he hit another ball further up the tree. 'Some shot you are!' I tell him. 'Too bad you can't see outta both eyes.' I aim at the red ball, and I miss too. The both of us pop BBs at that tree, and pretty soon the floor is covered with broken glass. Then Mario's mother walks in. First she shakes Mario till his brains rattle. Next she drags me home, scolding the whole way, and hands me over to my mother. For a week I don't sit down, and for a month I'm not allowed to use that BB gun."

Eddie grinned, considering Pop's story. A pot of geraniums blazed on a nearby porch. Eddie whipped out an imaginary revolver and snapped off three shots: Pow! Pow! Pow! Scarlet petals exploded into the air.

The next day, Eddie noticed something as he and Pop started up the block. Pop wasn't dragging his right leg so much and he had more energy. Mom was right—these walks had done Pop good. "Pop, you said something yesterday. About living in Brooklyn. You mean Brooklyn, New York?"

"Where else is Brooklyn gonna be?"

"I thought you lived your whole life in Philadelphia."

Pop made a gruff noise in the back of his throat. "I was born in Italy, Eddie. Came to America when I was seven. Lived in Brooklyn till I was eighteen."

Eddie had always known Pop was Italian, but he'd never realized that meant Pop was born in Italy. Eddie was as shocked as though he'd opened a door in his own house and discovered an unknown room. "Why did your family leave Italy?"

"No rain. Crops dried up. Leave Italy or starve, that's how it was. So we came to America—my parents, my brother Nick, baby Rosa, and me. Lived in one room, the five of us, till Papa and Nick found work. When we moved into a three-room apartment, we thought we was rich."

"Why did you move away from Brooklyn?"

Pop stopped and put his hand on a fence post. "When I graduated high school, my Uncle Sal offered me work in his barbershop in Philadelphia. Jobs was hard to come by, so I was glad of the opportunity. After Uncle Sal died, my Aunt Isabella sold me the house and barbershop. I been there ever since."

At the dinner table that night, Pop once again mentioned going home. "I been away too long, Don. I'm worried about Mama Z's fig tree. She'd never forgive me if anything happened to that tree."

81

"You don't have to worry about the fig tree," Dad assured him. "Joe makes sure it's watered. Isn't that right, Diane?"

"Joe's a good man," Pop said impatiently. "But it's time I went home and took care of my own place."

"Anybody want more french fries?" said Mom.

"Mickey, honey, how'd your swimming lesson go?" asked Dad.

Eddie scooped up a forkful of meat loaf. You didn't have to be a rocket scientist to see that Dad and Mom were putting Pop off. They figured he wasn't ready yet to return to Del Monte Street.

That night Eddie was stretched out on his bed reading a comic book when Pop began to undress. Eddie tossed aside the comic and rolled onto the floor to unlace Pop's shoes. "Pop, I was wondering, did you meet Mama Z in Phildalphia?"

Pop planted his gnarled hands on his knees, his mouth softening. "Now there's a story, Eddie. I used to see this girl walk past the barbershop, going to Castelli's Market up the street. Pretty as a ripe plum Carmela was, with long black hair and a waist so tiny I thought I could put my two hands around it."

"How did you get to know her?"

"One afternoon when I don't have no customer, I'm standing in the doorway enjoying the sunshine and Carmela walks by. I say hello. Carmela, she looks at me under her eyelashes, shy as a little bird, and says hello back."

"Then you asked for a date and pretty soon you got married."

"Eddie, you move too fast! First, I got to go to her house and meet her parents. We sit on the stoop in the evening, with her younger brothers and sisters hanging around. Sometimes we walk to Giovanni's ice cream parlor or go to a dance in the church hall. Finally I have some money saved, and I speak to her parents, ask permission to marry her."

"Things sure have changed, Pop." Eddie sat back on his heels. "People don't ask permission to get married these days."

"I don't know whether that's better or worse, Eddie. All I know is, Mama Z and me, we lived together on Del Monte Street for fifty-eight years. And all of them years was happy."

The next two days a drizzling rain fell, soaking the yard and trickling down the gutters. Pop spent his days in front of the TV set and spoke little at dinner. On the third day, watery sunlight broke through. Eddie hunted up his mother. "Want me to take Pop for a walk?"

"If you can get him moving." His mother rolled her eyes. "You'll need a chisel to pry him out of that chair."

When Eddie stood in front of the TV screen, Pop blinked at him like a bear coming out of hibernation. "Hey Pop, want to go for a walk?"

Pop looked toward the window. "Sounds good to me. I'm sick of sitting here."

As they started down the front walk, Eddie saw

Mom at the kitchen window, her mouth ajar. He grinned and flicked a thumbs-up sign.

"Yo, Eddie." Beanie rolled alongside on his bike, his maroon Phillies cap tipped backward on his head. "Mr. Zitelli, how you feeling?"

"Frisky as a mountain goat, Beanie. Watch out I don't steal your bike and ride off to Philadelphia."

"We're going for a walk," Eddie told Beanie. "Come along."

Beanie parked his bike on the lawn and trotted after them. Eddie tried to think of a way to start Pop spinning memories again. "Did you own a bike when you were a kid, Pop?"

"We lived in a three-room apartment on the fifth floor. Where was I gonna keep a bike? Besides I had no time for bike riding. Before I'm nine, I'm working every afternoon and all day Saturday."

"Before you were nine? I thought it was against the law for little kids to work."

"Back then, if you was big enough to walk, you was big enough to work."

"Where did you work, Mr. Zitelli?" asked Beanie.

"Corner candy store. I swept the sidewalk. Put magazines on the shelves. Washed windows."

"How about Nick?" Eddie asked. "What kind of job did he have?"

"Nicky found a job working in a bakery making bread. My father, he had the hardest time finding work. In Italy he was a farmer. In Brooklyn there were no farms. You know what my father expected to see when he came to America, Beanie? Streets paved with gold."

"You're pulling my leg, Mr. Zitelli."

"I'm telling you the truth. Back in Italy, all the churches had statues decorated with gold. So my father believed what people told him, that in America people were so rich the cobblestones were covered with gold. When we arrived in New York, he saw that wasn't true. Some streets was just mud, no paving at all. And Papa found work helping to pave them."

"How come I never met your brother Nick?" Eddie asked.

"Nicky died in a fire at the bakery when he was twenty-two. Rosa, she caught diphtheria. Died when she was twelve."

That would be like having Tony die. Or Mickey. Eddie broke a leaf from a hedge and split it with his thumbnail. "I told Beanie about your BB gun, Pop. You got any other stories about you and Mario?"

"Lemme see . . ." Pop tugged his ear, a grin tilting the corners of his mouth. "You boys ever heard of the Brooklyn Bridge? Prettiest bridge in the world. From my bedroom window I could see that bridge, strung with silver cables like some kind of giant harp. I used to think how wonderful Brooklyn would look from the top. Finally I made up my mind I was gonna climb up one of them big cables."

They'd reached the corner, but Pop stepped off the curb and continued across the street, still talking.

"Mario liked the idea, so one Sunday afternoon we started out to do it. People walked across that bridge all the time to save carfare, so nobody took no notice of two kids. We come to the place where the cable begins, the big one that goes to the top of the tower. Quick like a monkey, I hop the fence with Mario right behind me and we start up. I'm moving nice and easy, watching my feet, sliding my hands along the guide wires, when all of a sudden someone shouts: 'You kids! Get offa there.' I glance back, see a cop at the bottom of the cable shaking his nightstick at us. Mario gives me a push. 'Keep moving,' he says.

"For the first time, I look up where I'm headed, toward the top of the tower. Fat clouds are sliding behind the bridge, and it looks like the towers are falling over, gonna topple right into the East River. My head starts to spin, and I can't move. 'Andiamo, Corky. Let's go!' Mario yells. But I'm stuck, like my feet are glued down.

"Then the cop shouts again, closer now because he's coming after us. That sound breaks me loose because cops scare me worse than any bridge falling over. I scramble up the cable with Mario on my heels. We run across the platform, down the other side, and beat it back to Brooklyn like the devil's chasing us with a pitchfork."

"What happened to the policeman?" Eddie asked.

"For all I know, he's still stuck on that cable." Pop's chuckle rattled in his chest. "Listen, my legs is tired. Lemme sit on that bench and rest a minute."

No wonder Pop was tired. They'd walked all the way to Center Street. Pop patted the slats of the wooden bench. "What's a bench doing on this corner anyway?"

"Bus stop," said Eddie.

"Where do these buses go?"

"Philadelphia and down to the shore. Mom keeps a schedule in the kitchen drawer, but we hardly ever use the bus."

Pop made a gruff noise. "Everywhere you go, you ride a bike or climb into a car. You're lazy, you small-town kids! Don't know how to walk the way city kids do." Pop braced his hands on the bench and pushed himself to his feet. "Okay, I'm ready to start back."

Pop went past the front walk to the breezeway door. Inside the empty kitchen a pot simmered on the stove, giving off a spicy aroma of oregano and tomato. "Fix me a glass of water, will you, Eddie?" said Pop. "I'm gonna sit here and drink it."

Eddie gave Pop his glass of water and went back outside with Beanie. "Your grandfather has great stories," Beanie said. "Imagine climbing one of those cables! That took a lot of nerve."

It was weird, Eddie thought. He'd learned more about Pop in the past couple of days than he'd learned in all the years before that.

Mom served spaghetti and meatballs for dinner. Pop cleaned his plate. "Diane, you made a fine meal."

Mom's eyes glittered with pleasure. "Thanks, Pop, but I'll never match Mama Z's spaghetti."

"You remember the first time you came to Del Monte Street for dinner?"

"How could I forget?" Mom shook her head. "In

my house, Sunday dinner meant three of us sitting at that long mahogany table, my dad at one end carving the roast, my mother at the other end serving vegetables. When Don brought me to your house, I thought you were having a party. All those people crowded around the table—you and Mama Z, Father Charles, Tess, Sal. Knees and elbows bumping, everybody talking at once, and those good smells in the air! Then Tess and Mama Z began to serve dinner."

"Antipasto first," said Dad.

"With provolone and salami and anchovies—I'd never even *seen* an anchovy before. And that delicious hard bread to wipe up the juice."

"Spaghetti next," Dad prompted.

"And a big bowl of sausage and Mama Z's special meatballs. I wanted to be polite so I ate till I thought I'd burst. Then Mama Z said, 'Tess, you put on clean plates while I bring in the dinner.' I couldn't believe it—roast chicken, peas, mashed potatoes. Another whole meal!"

"Then dessert."

"Pastry from Roselli's Bakery."

"And coffee—"

"With a splash of anisette. Finally Mama Z carried in a tray of roasted chestnuts. I thought I'd never stand on my feet again!"

Pop was nodding, his eyes bright. "Soon as I go home, we're gonna have a Sunday dinner like that. You can cook the spaghetti, Diane. I'll buy bread and pastry from Roselli's."

Mom's glance caught Dad's and flicked away. "Those Sunday dinners, they were good, Pop," Dad said. "Nice to hang on to those memories." He drained his coffee mug and set it down. "The grass has dried off. Tony, you can mow the lawn tonight. Eddie, you do the trimming."

Eddie looked from Dad to Mom, the truth settling into his brain. At last he understood the real reason why his parents changed the subject every time Pop talked about going home. Mom and Dad didn't expect Pop to return to Del Monte Street. Not ever.

"Eddie, did you remember that I'm going to the shore with Mickey's Brownie troop tomorrow?" said Mom. "You promised you'd be around in case Pop needs anything."

Eddie expected Pop to growl that he didn't need a nursemaid, but Pop only said mildly, "Don't worry, Diane. Eddie and me, we'll do fine."

Later Eddie realized that he should have caught on right then, should have known that Pop was hatching a plot. But when he ambled into the bedroom that night, Eddie had no clue that something was brewing.

Pop was in bed, but still awake. He waved Eddie over and said in a papery whisper, "Tomorrow I'm taking the bus to Philadelphia. Eddie, I want you to go with me."

Chapter 11

The next morning, Eddie awoke with a jolt. He heard the bathroom door open, shut, and open again. Mickey's light footsteps padded toward the kitchen. In a few minutes, a car rolled out the driveway and faded up the street.

Across the room, Pop flung back the covers. He limped over to Eddie, his striped pajamas hanging in loose folds. "Time to get moving, Eddie."

"I hear you, Pop."

As Eddie dressed, uneasiness buzzed in his chest like a fly in a fruit jar. Dad and Mom were gone for sure. But what if Tony came in to talk with Pop before leaving for work and asked how Pop and Eddie planned to spend the day?

Cool it, Eddie told himself. Tony hadn't dropped in yet to chat with Pop.

While Eddie was in the bathroom, the garage door

grated up. Eddie darted into Mickey's bedroom and peered out the window. Tony was coasting down the drive on his bike.

"Tony just left," Eddie reported to Pop. "The coast is clear."

Pop was dressed and sitting on the edge of the bed, hair combed, face alert. "I'm ready," he said.

"You sure you feel up to this, Pop? Climbing into a bus and tramping around Philadelphia?"

"I feel wonderful, Eddie. And I know what I'm doing. I planned in my head how I'm gonna manage everything."

Still Eddie hesitated. "You promise"—his voice twanged nervously, like an overtightened guitar string—"you promise we're just going for a visit? You'll come right back to New Jersey?"

"Eddie, I only want to see the house and the shop, make sure everything's okay. Plus I need to take care of a little business. We'll be back long before your mother gets home."

We better be, Eddie thought as he followed Pop to the kitchen for breakfast. Mom and Dad would french-fry Eddie if they found out about this trip. But how could Eddie refuse to accompany Pop after Pop had bailed him out of his jam with the storm door?

The bright morning sun promised midday heat. Pop struck off briskly along the sidewalk. At the bus stop, a woman sat on the bench reading a paperback novel. "Looks like you're right about the bus," Eddie told Pop.

"You think I don't know how to read a timetable?" said Pop. "Here comes the bus now."

When the door whooshed open, Eddie chewed his lip nervously. Could Pop climb up that high step?

"Gimme a push," Pop ordered, gripping the railing. Eddie braced his hands against Pop's back, and Pop swung up into the bus.

As the bus lurched away from the curb, Pop wobbled off balance, and a black man wearing jeans and a striped T-shirt reached up to grab his arm. Pop bobbed his head in thanks. "Haven't ridden a bus for a while," he explained cheerfully. "I'm outta practice."

As they settled themselves in an empty seat, Pop whispered out of the corner of his mouth, "We made a clean getaway, eh, Eddie?"

Eddie caught the spark of mischief in Pop's faded eyes. Easy for Pop to say. It would be Eddie's neck on the chopping block if he and Pop were caught.

The bus passed through more small towns, picking up additional passengers. Then they veered onto the expressway leading to the Delaware River. In the distance Eddie saw the blue towers of the Walt Whitman Bridge. Eddie shuddered. No way would he climb one of those cables!

On the Pennsylvania side, the bus turned onto Broad Street. Brick row houses slid past. A funeral parlor. Fast-food restaurants. A bank.

Pop nudged Eddie. "Next stop we get off."

The black man exited from the bus ahead of them. He waited on the sidewalk as Eddie edged past Pop and swung down onto the curb. How in blazes was Pop going to manage that drop? "Let me give you a hand," said the man. Together, he and Eddie balanced Pop down onto the sidewalk. "Take it light, brother," the man told Pop with a smile.

Pop put his hand on the wire trash container on the corner, his breath jerking in and out. "You okay?" Eddie asked anxiously.

"Lemme rest a minute, I'll be fine. I ain't jumped off too many buses lately." Pop nodded at the sign above them. "Lombard Street. Right where we want to be. Okay, Eddie, let's go."

They walked for several blocks with Pop padding along beside Eddie, taking Eddie's arm to go up and down at curbs. "Next corner's Ninth Street. We'll walk over to Del Monte through Ninth Street market."

"What's Ninth Street market?"

Pop shot Eddie a surprised look. "You mean you never been there? How could a grandson of mine grow up I never took him to the Ninth Street market?"

Easy. When they were little and visited Philadelphia often, Tony was the one Pop took places. Later, after Tess and her family moved to Cincinnati and especially after Mama Z took sick, she and Pop mostly came to Eddie's house for visits.

They walked several blocks on Ninth Street. At one side street a truck with slatted sides was parked beside a loading platform. A chorus of bleats leaked through the slats. Sheep. Or maybe goats, Eddie figured.

Pop quickened his pace, and Eddie looked ahead curiously. In the next block, wooden stands piled with fresh produce lined the gutters, and people thronged the street and sidewalks. Pop nudged Eddie. "Not much like the grocery store where your mother shops, eh, Eddie?"

Not at all like Mom's air-conditioned supermarket. Here everything was in the open—pyramids of oranges and lemons, heaps of pale green lettuce, mounds of shiny red and green peppers, wooden crates holding apples, pears, and plums nestled in tissue paper. The hucksters behind the stands chanted as they worked: "Get your tomatoes, three pounds for a dollar . . ." "Cantaloupe, sweet and juicy, who wants a cantaloupe? . . ." "Onions, I got onions. . . ." Scales swung and paper bags crackled.

"Hey, Corky! How the hell are you?" called a curly-haired man in a sleeveless undershirt.

"Ready to take on the world, Dominic!"

Even the stores along Ninth Street displayed merchandise outside: wicker baskets, straw mats hung over metal racks, T-shirts stacked on long tables. In front of one store, an Oriental woman with almond-shaped eyes arranged pocketbooks on hooks beneath the store's striped awning. "Good morning, Mrs. Chen," called Pop, and the woman's moon-shaped face plumped into a smile. "Mista Zitelli, velly nice to see you!"

No wonder Pop missed this place. These people knew him. Pop fitted here like a pit in a peach.

The crowd was too thick to walk two abreast, so Eddie dropped behind Pop. A black teenager passed, pushing a rack of dresses. Behind a produce stand, a boy about Eddie's age was piling up sacks of onions. A skinny kid, maybe eight or nine, worked his way along the sidewalk, calling out: "Shopping bags, who needs a shopping bag?" In the Ninth Street market, even kids were allowed to work, Eddie thought enviously.

He smelled fresh-baked bread and saw a bakery window filled with crusty loaves, jam-filled cookies, and sugar-powdered pastry. Next door, a sign on a luncheonette boasted BEST CHEESE STEAKS IN PHILADELPHIA. Eddie sniffed the rich aroma of fried onions.

He sidestepped an island of wooden crates that occupied the middle of the sidewalk. Ducks hissed and quacked behind the open slats. The window of the nearby store held chicken pieces mounded on beds of crushed ice. In the next store window, silver fish and pale scallops were arranged on similar beds of ice.

Ahead, Pop waited at the corner, his hand against a telephone pole. An alarm went off in Eddie's head when he saw Pop's sallow face and the beads of perspiration on his forehead. "Are you all right?" Eddie demanded.

"A little dizzy, that's all. It's okay. We're gonna sit down soon."

Pop veered up the side street, wobbly as a windup toy with a broken spring. Eddie grabbed his arm to steady him.

"We're going in here." Pop nodded toward a doorway. Baffled Eddie studied the maroon awning above the white entrance where white script spelled out: RISTORANTE LA SCALA. They'd eaten breakfast before they left, and it was barely ten-thirty. What the heck did Pop want with a restaurant?

Chapter 12

Inside, darkness closed around Eddie like an under-water cave. Tables draped with white linen floated over the wine red carpet. Behind the polished bar, a boy about Tony's age was wiping glasses. He had heavy-lidded eyes and a wing of dark hair over his forehead.

"We don't open for lunch till eleven-thirty," the boy called.

Pop hauled himself toward the bar, his weak leg dragging clumsily. "Are you Maria's son?"

The boy nodded.

"I want to see your Uncle Frank. Tell him it's Corky Zitelli."

The boy disappeared through a doorway. In a moment he returned with a husky man wearing dark slacks and a white shirt open at the neck.

"Corky!" The man wrapped his heavy fingers around Pop's hand. "Good to see you. Georgie, why didn't you give Mr. Zitelli a chair?" He pulled out a chair for Pop at one of the tables, then settled himself opposite. "You'd like a soda, Corky? Or a glass of wine?"

"Just a little water, Frank. With some ice maybe."

"Bring us two glasses of water," Frank called, then turned to Eddie. "You want a soda, right? Kids always want soda. Corky, this is one of Don's boys. Gotta be." Frank's eyes, hooded by the same heavy lids as Georgie's, swept Eddie up and down, and the full mouth creased into a smile. "In a couple of years, anybody causes trouble with this grandson of yours is gonna regret it." He crossed his arms on the table and leaned forward. "Now, what can I do for you?"

Pop began to speak in Italian. Eddie, drinking his soda at the bar, couldn't understand a word. When Pop finished, Frank took a long swallow from his glass of water. Then he answered in Italian, his voice low. At the end, he turned his palms up. "You understand, Corky, sometimes these things go wrong."

"I got confidence in you, Frank," Pop said with dignity.

They stood up, and Frank put his arm across Pop's shoulder. "It's okay to call you at Don's house?"

"Ask for Eddie. He'll take the message."

"This Eddie, he's your right-hand man, eh?"

No, thought Eddie, Tony was Pop's right-hand man. But all Pop said was, "Listen, Frank, I appreciate this."

"Hey"—Frank squeezed Pop's shoulder—"how

many years my family owes you? At last you let us do something."

Outside, blinking in the sunlight, Eddie turned Frank's words over in his head. "You did a favor for that guy's family, Pop?"

"Two men came to my barbershop looking for Frank's father. I sent word to his family these men was hunting for him."

"That was the whole favor?"

"These men had guns, Eddie. Frank's father, he left town in a hurry."

Eddie plodded along the sidewalk, questions bursting inside his head like firecrackers. "Pop—"

"No more." Pop brushed the air with his hand. "I don't want to talk no more about it."

The noise from Ninth Street market dwindled as they rounded the corner onto a quiet street of brick row houses with marble steps at each front door and metal awnings shading the first-floor windows. Eddie recognized Del Monte Street.

Pop stumped along, his energy renewed. Near the end of the block he grunted with pleasure and veered toward an elderly blue Chevy parked by the curb. Pop tried the car doors and gave a nod of satisfaction when he found the windows open at the top to let the heat escape.

"We'll go in through the shop," Pop said, pointing to the barber pole at the corner.

Eddie trailed Pop through the glass-paneled door

101

into the aroma of hair oil and shaving cream. A wiry man in a green barber's jacket was trimming a customer's hair.

"Joe," Pop called, "you got time to give me a haircut?"

Joe Salvatore dropped his comb and scissors on the counter and clapped Pop on the shoulder. "Corky, what a surprise! You're a sight to make the birdies sing."

"Why didn't you let us know you were coming?" said the man in the barber chair, reaching for Pop's hand. "You think I'd have let this butcher touch my hair if I could have had a haircut from you?"

"Vito, I'm sorry. I'll maybe be here for your next haircut."

Eddie saw the flash of surprise in Joe Salvatore's eyes. Clearly Joe didn't expect Pop to come back to live on Del Monte Street either.

"How did you get here, Corky? Don drive you over?"

"Eddie and me, we took the bus. I just wanted to look around the house. See how things are going."

"Sure, sure. Vito, I'll be right back."

Joe led the way through the curtained doorway into the small storage room at the rear of the barbershop. "Everything's in good shape," Joe assured Pop as he unlocked the door in the opposite wall. "Nobody goes in but me. And Diane, of course, the day she came to pick up your clothes. Every morning, I walk through the house top to bottom. Make sure everything's okay."

"I saw the car. It looks good."

"I run the engine a couple times a week. You got no problems with that car. Corky, you're really coming back? You think you can manage here on your own?"

"I'll need help with the laundry and cooking, that's all."

Joe hesitated, fingering the door key. "Vito's niece, she's looking for work."

"Sounds good. But don't mention it yet. First I have to make some arrangements."

Pop limped past Joe with Eddie on his heels. The door shut behind them, and they stood in the dining room of Pop's house.

On the left, a stairway rose to the living room and the bedrooms on the upper floors. In the center of the room was the heavy dining room table, covered with a lace tablecloth. A long mirror, wavery with age, hung on the opposite wall. In it Eddie saw the ghostly images of himself and Pop. What was Pop thinking? Did he imagine Mama Z pushing through the door from the kitchen, a steaming platter of food in her hands? Did he hear the hum of voices as the family gathered here for Sunday dinner?

Pop shook himself like an old dog rousing from a nap. "Come on, Eddie," he said and stumped toward the kitchen.

Eddie had never seen the kitchen this tidy. No teakettle steaming on the stove, no bananas ripening in the basket on the table, no chopping board with bits of green pepper or onion flying under Mama Z's swift knife. Only bars of sunlight falling through the window

103

over the sink, fine specks of dust floating in the pale glow.

Pop leaned close to the window, craning to see into the handkerchief-sized backyard. "Fig tree looks fine," he said with satisfaction. Eddie knew why that was important. Pop had planted that fig tree the day he and Mama Z returned from their honeymoon in Atlantic City.

Pop opened a cupboard and studied the bare shelves. "Gonna need groceries," he said to himself.

Swinging around, Pop returned to the dining room. "Whoa!" Eddie protested as he realized that Pop was headed for the stairway. "You can't climb those stairs."

"Eddie, this is my house," Pop said firmly. "Here, I make the rules."

Dismayed, Eddie followed as Pop hauled himself up the stairway, wheezing hard, every step a struggle. At the top, he jerked around to face Eddie, his faded eyes triumphant. "I made it."

Yeah, thought Eddie. With me behind you in case you lost your balance. Mom was right. Pop could never manage alone in this house.

Pop shuffled toward the living room, but Eddie paused a moment, his attention caught by the sepia-toned photograph on the wall at the head of the stairs. Pop and Mama Z's wedding portrait.

Eddie had never paid much attention to this picture before. Pop faced the camera, a short, slender young man dressed in a dark suit, his face stiff and self-conscious. Studying Pop's wavy hair, wide-set dark eyes, and straight nose, Eddie saw why everybody said Tony was the spitting image of Pop. Mama Z sat in a carved wooden chair, a shy-looking girl wearing a white dress, a ruff of veil covering her hair, the ribbons from her bouquet of flowers trailing around her slim ankles and pointed slippers. *Pretty as a ripe plum Carmela was, with long black hair and a waist so tiny I thought I could put my two hands around it.*

"Hey, your legs stopped working?"

Eddie jerked back to reality. "Coming, Pop."

In the living room, crocheted doilies lay like lily pads on the plush sofa and overstuffed armchairs. Family photographs crowded the end tables: Eddie's dad, a serious little kid with jug-handle ears wearing his First Communion suit; Tess grinning and waving a rolled-up diploma the day she graduated from high school; Father Charles, newly ordained, with Pop and Mama Z on either side of him, their faces wreathed in smiles.

Pop touched the curled ivy on the coffee table, and a dry leaf broke off in his fingers. "That's the last of Carmela's plants," he said.

He left the living room and clumped down the hall to the back bedroom. Peering over Pop's shoulder, Eddie saw the double bed Pop and Mama Z had shared, dipping at the center into the comfortable hollow Eddie remembered from Sunday afternoon naps when he was small. The air still held the faint scent of Mama Z's talcum powder and the mothballs she had sprinkled on closet floors.

"Eddie, I'm gonna take this picture back to New

Jersey. Carry it for me, will you?" Pop lifted a photograph from his bureau—Father Charles, Aunt Tess, and Eddie's dad gathered around Pop and Mama Z on their fiftieth wedding anniversary.

They returned to the hall, and Pop glanced at the flight of stairs leading to the third-floor bedrooms. "Not up there," protested Eddie.

Pop shook his head. "I got other things to do. Help me down the stairs, Eddie."

Going down was even tougher than going up. Pop clung to the banister with his good hand, and Eddie squeezed along the wall on the other side, gripping Pop's arm. Each time Pop lurched down a step, Eddie's heart bucked in his chest. "If you fall," he muttered through clenched teeth, "drag me with you so I don't have to face Mom and Dad."

"I . . . ain't . . . gonna . . . fall," Pop grunted.

At the bottom, Eddie pulled out a chair, and Pop sank onto it, his breath whistling in his chest. "Time to start back?" Eddie asked hopefully.

"I gotta do one more thing."

"What's that?"

"I gotta go down the cellar."

"Are you nuts? No way. You'd break your neck!"

Pop's voice ground out, low and stubborn. "Eddie, I'm going."

"Come on, Pop! I can take care of anything you want done down there."

Pop shook his head, and Eddie threw up his hands in anger. "You're as stubborn as ten mules! And I'm the one who'll be tarred and feathered if anything happens to you."

Pop pushed himself up from the chair. "Eddie, I gotta go down the cellar. You can help me, or I'll go alone."

Eddie argued the whole way into the kitchen, but Pop paid no attention. "All right!" Eddie banged his fist on the table. "You'll have to sit down."

"What do you mean?"

"You'll have to sit down to do it. Slide down the stairs on your butt."

Briefly Pop's face furrowed into a net of angry wrinkles. Then he burst out laughing. "You know what? You got a great idea."

Not great, but the best Eddie could come up with. With Eddie's help, Pop seated himself on the top stair, then worked his way down the flight of rickety wooden steps. Eddie backed ahead of him, ready to assist if needed. At the bottom, Eddie pulled Pop to his feet.

"You wait in the kitchen," said Pop. "I'll call you when I'm ready."

Eddie stamped up the stairs and flung himself onto a kitchen chair. Stubborn old coot! No wonder he drove Mom crazy. Pop's brain ran on one track, and heaven help anybody standing on the rails.

What did Pop want in that cellar anyway? Low-ceilinged and dusty, it was strung with clotheslines and crowded with discarded baby carriages, piles of old newspaper, broken snow shovels, and unwanted furniture. Mom was right. Pop and Mama Z had kept every single thing they brought into this house during their entire married life.

Eddie looked at the clock over the refrigerator. Quarter after twelve. The long walk to the bus stop still lay ahead, then the wait for a bus to carry them back to New Jersey. What if Mom or Dad beat them home? Ice water flowed down Eddie's spine. "Pop, you ready?" he called.

"Come down and get me," Pop replied from the cellar.

Back in the kitchen, Pop sat on a chair until his breathing slowed and the scarlet blotches faded from his cheeks. "I'm gonna say good-bye to Joe. Then we'll leave by the kitchen door."

Eddie paced the kitchen, scowling at the clock, until Pop returned, a shabby leather key case in his hand. He locked the kitchen door carefully after they went out.

Heat shimmered up from the sidewalk, and the weight of the midday sun pressed down. Remembering the long trek to the bus stop, Eddie said, "Maybe we should call a taxi."

"We don't need no taxi." Pop held up the key case. "I'm gonna drive us back to New Jersey."

Chapter 13

"No way, Pop!" Eddie protested. "If you show up with that car, Mom and Dad will know we've been in Philadelphia. And they'll kill me!"

Ignoring Eddie, Pop unlocked the passenger door, then walked around to the driver's side. "Eddie, get in." Frustrated, Eddie flung himself into the car beside Pop.

"Wind down your window. We don't want to melt."

Why not? thought Eddie. He was about to be boiled in oil anyway.

The ride to the bridge increased Eddie's terror. Trolley rails caught the car wheels, making the Chevy shimmy like half-set gelatin. Taxis sped through yellow lights, and pedestrians crossing at intersections brushed the hood of the car.

Leaving the bridge in New Jersey, Pop leaned close to the wheel, squinting at the road. "I ain't driven in

New Jersey for a while. Watch the signs, Eddie. Give me some help."

At last they reached Belvidere. Pop gunned the car up the driveway and swerved onto the grass under the maple tree. Eddie stared through the dusty windshield, unable to move.

Tony strode out the breezeway door and came toward the car, astonishment scrawled across his face. "What's going on? Where the heck have you two been?"

"We went—" Eddie's voice came out in a squeak. He stared at Tony, leaning on the door beside him. "We went to Philadelphia. To Del Monte Street."

Tony shook his head. "Pop, you are a fox!" In a whisper, he added to Eddie, "And you'll be mincemeat when Mom and Dad find out."

Pop pushed down the door handle and got out. "I'm hungry. We got anything to eat around here?"

While Eddie fixed a sandwich for Pop, Tony asked Pop questions. Pop told about catching the bus, walking through the Ninth Street market, and visiting Del Monte Street, but he never mentioned La Scala Restaurant or the man named Frank. Finally Pop raised a trembling hand. "No more, Tony, I'm tired. I'm gonna rest now."

Pop's legs scraped like rusty pliers as Eddie helped him to the bedroom and pulled back the spread. Lying down, Pop looked up at Eddie, his face creased with fatigue. "You're a good boy, Eddie."

Eddie mumbled something, thinking that Pop might be grateful but Dad and Mom would be furious.

Dad arrived home at four-thirty. Eddie heard the car and hurried to the kitchen. Through the window, Eddie saw his father walking around the Chevy, his face as puzzled as if he'd found a flying saucer parked in the front yard.

Then Mom's car pulled into the drive. Mickey hopped out and Mom followed, both of them flushed with sunburn. Mom stared in disbelief at the Chevy. "What in the world . . . ? Is that Pop's car?"

Tony spoke over Eddie's shoulder. "Ready for the slaughter?"

Mickey, Mom, and Dad came through the breezeway door. "How did Pop's car get here?" Dad demanded.

"Don't look at me," said Tony with a shrug.

Eddie licked his lips. "Pop went to Philadelphia and drove the car back. He asked me to go along."

He heard Mom's sharp intake of breath. "How did you get to Philadelphia?" Dad asked.

"On the bus."

"You took Pop to Philadelphia on the bus?" Mom put her hand on her chest.

"What did you do in the city?"

Eddie clenched and unclenched his fingers. Pop hadn't told Tony about La Scala. Was that a secret?

"Pop wanted to visit the house, didn't he?" Dad went on.

Relieved, Eddie nodded. "Joe Salvatore was in the barbershop cutting some guy's hair. He and Pop talked, then Pop went in to look the house over."

"I told Pop everything was fine," Mom burst out. "I told him Joe was taking care of things."

"He needed to see for himself, Diane, can't you understand that? What did Pop tell Joe?"

"That pretty soon he'd be back home for good."

"I knew it. I knew it!"

"Pop doesn't really expect to go back, Diane. He's just saying that so he can give himself time to come to grips with the situation."

"You're wrong, Dad," Eddie put in. "Pop does expect to go home"

His father turned his palms up. "Well, maybe he will. Maybe Pop will do better than the doctor expects."

"I can't believe what I'm hearing." Mom folded her arms. "The doctor said no stairs, and you talk as if it's reasonable for Pop to live in a three-story house."

"We can move a bed downstairs. He can sleep in the dining room."

"Will you move the bathroom downstairs too? And who's going to cook and do the laundry?"

"Pop's going to hire somebody," Eddie said. "Some man named Vito has a daughter who wants a job."

"Will Vito's wonderful daughter come seven days a week? What happens when she's sick or needs a day off?"

"Diane, you're crossing bridges we haven't come to."

"Who crossed those bridges when Mama Z was sick?

It's fine for you to skim over those hard realities, Don. You're not the one who drove to Philadelphia for eight months to do laundry and take Mama Z for chemotherapy and pick up prescriptions and handle medical bills. Now there's a tough nut for you to crack—paying the bills. By what magic do you expect Pop to come up with money to pay a housekeeper? Or have you and Tess discovered a gold mine I don't know about so that you can hire a housekeeper for him?" Mom's voice broke off, leaving a jagged silence.

Dad jerked his thumb at the children. "Out!"

"What are Mom and Dad fighting about?" Mickey whispered as they pushed through the doorway.

"Pop won't face facts," said Tony. "And bean-brain here is helping Pop blow soap bubbles."

Eddie jerked away from his brother. So Tony had guessed. Right from the beginning, Tony had realized that Mom and Dad expected Pop to stay for good. But Pop didn't want to live here. He wanted to return to his own house.

Eddie walked into the bedroom, his feelings like snarled fish lines. Pop, awake from his nap, was sitting in the rocker. "I heard your parents pull in. Turn around. Go on, Eddie, turn around. I don't see no blood. Any broken bones?"

Crazy old guy. A grin wobbled across Eddie's face. "Mom and Dad started arguing and forgot about me."

"Did you mention La Scala?"

Eddie shook his head.

"Good boy." Pop beckoned Eddie closer, and his

113

voice sank to a whisper. "A phone call's gonna come for me. You take it. Somebody will give you a message and you write it down, no mistakes, okay?"

Nothing doing. Eddie wanted no more of Pop's schemes. But before he could answer, Mickey put her head round the door. "Beanie's on the phone. In Mom and Dad's bedroom."

Eddie hurried to the phone. "Dad got paid and Mom's celebrating. She bought a steak as big as Texas. Want to come to dinner?"

"Hold on a minute, Beanie." Eddie put his hand over the receiver as Mom and Dad filed into the bedroom, their faces drained.

"It's Beanie," Eddie said. "Asking me to dinner." He waited to hear his mother retort, Are you out of your mind? After the stupid thing you did today?

"What?" Mom looked at him vaguely. "Oh . . . I guess so." She sat on the side of the bed and began to unbuckle her sandals.

"I'll be right over, Beanie," Eddie whispered hastily.

He hung up the phone and edged toward the door. But Dad put a hand on his shoulder. "That trip to Philadelphia was crazy, Eddie. If Pop wanted to see the house, he should have asked your mother or me to drive him."

"I know why he didn't ask me," Mom said, slipping off her sandals. "I wouldn't have let him bring the Chevy back."

"Diane, my father has owned just one car in his

whole life. If he wants to bring that Chevy to New Jersey and park it in our front yard so he can see for himself nobody's prying off the hubcaps, is that such a big deal?"

"I don't mind the car, Don. Or Pop wanting to visit Del Monte Street. But I feel as though I'm caught in the middle! You tell me to take care of Pop, make sure he follows the doctor's orders. I try, and Pop does as he pleases."

"Look, honey, we both know Pop has to change. He can't live alone on Del Monte Street. But Pop hasn't accepted that yet."

Mom bent down and rubbed her feet, her voice muffled. "I'm not sure you have either."

Dad turned to Eddie with a frown. "Pop maneuvered you into a tough spot today. If he comes up with any other wild notions, use your head, Eddie—let me know what's going on."

"I will, Dad. For sure."

In the hall, Eddie remembered the phone call Pop expected. Could it cause another problem? No, he told himself. After all, what harm could come of a phone call? Anyway, if trouble popped up, Eddie would do what he was supposed to do—turn the whole matter over to Dad.

Chapter 14

"Mickey, what do you call this?" Pop tugged the tassel of hair that swung from the crown of Mickey's head.

"A ponytail, Pop."

"Oh, yeah? Well, if that's a ponytail, you gotta be a pony."

It was the next day. Tony had gone to the mall with Joe. Eddie, Pop, Mickey, Mom, and Dad were sitting around the picnic table in the backyard. Patches of sun and shadow flickered across the crumpled napkins and crumb-strewn paper plates left from lunch.

Mickey pulled away from Pop and pranced across the yard, sunlight sparking on her glasses. "I am!" she cried. "I'm a pony, and I gallop around all day."

She skidded to a halt next to Pop, and he looped his arm around her waist. "Some day, little pony, I'll take you to see real horses—thoroughbreds—gallop around a track. Don, you go to the races much these days?"

"Haven't been at all lately, Pop."

"Remember the first time I took you and Charlie? Charlie was a senior in high school, and we bet ten bucks on a horse named Happy Homer because Charlie had hit a home run for the baseball team the day before."

Dad grinned. "That horse had never won a race in his life, and he came in by three lengths! I can still see Mama Z's face when you handed her that fistful of money."

"We had some good times at the track, you and Charlie and me. Be nice to go again."

"Why not? Why the heck not? I'll take an afternoon off, we'll hop in the car, drive down to Atlantic City. Have a glass of beer and bet a few bucks."

Mom put her hand on Dad's. "You know Pop's not allowed to drink beer."

"The beer I don't need, Diane. But an afternoon at the track, that sounds good."

The trip to Philadelphia had helped Pop, Eddie decided. He was mellow as a kid with a double-decker ice-cream cone today. He hadn't even turned prickly when Mom mentioned the doctor's orders.

"We'll go soon, Pop," Dad assured him.

Pop shook the ice cubes in the bottom of his glass. "No hurry, Don," he said mildly. "No hurry at all."

On Sunday Eddie and Beanie went fishing in Miller Park. They didn't catch anything, but they had fun trying. Monday Eddie finished the plane model he'd been working on. Summer was beginning to shape up after all.

On Tuesday, Eddie woke late to feel Tony's rough hand on his shoulder. "Must be nice," said Tony. "Sleep all day while the rest of us work. Pop's in the kitchen, Dad's at the office, and I'm off to the nursery. We're doing a landscaping job at a housing development in Fairboro. Mom's gone too. Grandmother Mayes phoned this morning. She strained her back or something, so Mom and Mickey drove up to visit her. Mom said to tell you there's stuff for lunch in the fridge and don't leave Pop alone." Tony turned his head, listening. "Phone. I'll get it."

Eddie kicked back the sheet. Shoot. He and Beanie had planned to head over to Ken's this morning. Ken had a new skateboard. Why was Mom so worried about leaving Pop alone?

Tony leaned through the door. "Phone's for you."

"Who is it?"

"Hey, I'm not your secretary. Find out for yourself."

Mom and Dad's bedroom was a mess, the bed unmade, clothes lying on chairs. Mom must have left in a hurry. Yawning, Eddie picked up the receiver.

"Is this Eddie Zitelli? I have a message for your grandfather."

Eddie's brain snapped fully awake. "Hold on a minute." He reached for the pad and pencil in the night table drawer. "Okay, what's the message?"

"A horse named Tia Two-Step is running in the third race at Atlantic City. The horse looks good. That's today, at Atlantic City, Tia Two-Step in the third." The connection broke.

Eddie stared at the pad. For pete's sake. This was the message Pop had been expecting—a tip on a horse race?

"Pop, your phone call came."

Pop laid down his toast. "That call was for me? Tell me what you heard, Eddie."

"A horse named Tia Two-Step is running in the third race at Atlantic City. The horse looks good. That's what the guy said—the horse looks good."

"The race is today?"

Eddie consulted the scrap of paper. "I guess so. Yeah, it's today."

Pop swung around to see the clock. "Third race goes off maybe three o'clock. Eddie, I gotta talk to your father."

"You want me to call him at work? Sure, Pop."

Eddie looked up Dad's work number, relieved. He wouldn't need to tell Dad about Pop's phone call—Pop was going to tell Dad himself.

"Core-Tech Data Systems."

"Extension seven-one-one, please."

"Marketing department."

"I'd like to speak with Mr. Zitelli."

"Mr. Zitelli isn't in the office at the moment. May I take a message?"

"This is his son Eddie. Do you know where my dad is?"

"He had an appointment with a client. He'll be back before lunch. Shall I have him call you when he comes in?"

"Yeah. Please."

Pop worked his lower lip between his fingers. "How long does it take to drive here from your father's office?"

"Maybe half an hour."

"To the track, another forty-five minutes." Pop studied the clock again. "First race goes off at two."

"You want Dad to come home and take you to the racetrack?"

"How else I'm gonna bet on that horse?"

"Can't you place a bet over the phone, with a bookie or something?"

"This bet I gotta make in person."

"Okay, Pop, no problem. Secretary said Dad'll be back before lunch. That will give you plenty of time to make the race."

Pop pushed away from the table. "I'm gonna shave and change my clothes. You stay near the phone, Eddie."

Eddie decided to rustle up some breakfast. The carton of Cocoa Crunchies faced him from the pantry shelf. Stupid cereal. Worst stuff Eddie had ever tasted, but Mom insisted that he finish the whole box.

Jake rubbed against Eddie's ankles, looking for a

handout. "How about a little bowl of cereal?" said Eddie.

Eddie shook Cocoa Crunchies into Jake's bowl and added a splash of Dad's coffee cream. Jake lapped up the cream and left the cereal. Even Jake knew a crummy product when he tasted it. Eddie dumped the soggy Cocoa Crunchies down the garbage disposal and fixed himself four slices of toast with butter and strawberry jam.

Pop returned to the kitchen, his cheeks scraped smooth and his sparse strands of gray hair slicked across his scalp. "Nothin' yet?"

"It's barely ten o'clock, Pop."

"I don't got all day to fool around. Listen, here's what we do next. I want to read about this Tia Two-Step, and your father's newspaper don't carry no racing page. I'll wait here for the phone call. You go buy me an *Inquirer*."

Eddie dressed and biked over to Center Street to buy the *Philadelphia Inquirer*. Skidding back up the driveway, he heard the phone. Clutching the newspaper, Eddie dropped his bike. leaped the azalea bushes, and burst through the breezeway door.

Pop had the phone to his ear. "Mickey ain't here," he told the caller. "She went somewhere with her mother." He hung up, scowling.

"It's still early," Eddie said.

"Lemme me see that paper." Pop laid the *Inquirer* on the kitchen table and flapped it open to the racing section.

Eddie bent over beside Pop to read the section on Atlantic City Racetrack. "Hey, here's your horse, Pop." He pointed to the line of print: *8 Tia Two-Step (Hanover) 113 20-1 Dull last four.* "What's all this stuff mean?"

"Horse is gonna start in eighth position off the rail. Hanover, that's the jockey's name. One hundred thirteen pounds is how much weight the horse will carry. And the odds are twenty to one. Every dollar you bet, the horse pays twenty."

"No kidding! Pop, you could clean up on this horse."

"First the horse has to win, Eddie. And Tia Two-Step is a long shot. 'Dull last four.' That means she looked bad her last four races."

"Why would anyone expect her to win today?"

The wrinkles in Pop's face tightened. "Sometimes people know things," he said.

"What kind of things?"

"Maybe the horse has been held back, and today the jockey's gonna let her run."

Didn't make sense. Why would anybody hold a horse back? Eddie studied the listings for the other races. "These horses sure have crazy names: Hairy Deal . . . Mama's Sons . . . All Shook Up."

"Mama's Sons? Show me that horse."

"Right here, Pop. In the first race."

Pop grinned so widely that the silver fillings in his back teeth showed. "I'm gonna put two dollars on that horse, Eddie. For Mama Z." Pop swung around in his chair to check the time.

123

"You'll wear that clock out, staring at it. Dad probably won't call before eleven-thirty. Go sit on the breezeway, Pop. Read the sports section. I'll wait here to answer the phone."

Eddie rinsed the dirty dishes and stacked them in the dishwasher. Then he read the comics section.

Quarter of twelve. Out on the porch Pop rattled the newspaper together. He shuffled inside and sat down in a chair that faced the clock, his thumb jerking against the tabletop.

"Listen, Pop, it's early for your lunch, but how about I make you a sandwich? Once you talk to Dad, he'll shoot right home, and the two of you will be flying off to the track."

"Good idea."

But Pop barely touched the ham-and-cheese sandwich Eddie fixed. "Look at the time, Eddie. Ten after twelve! Call your dad's office again. Maybe that secretary forgot to give him the message."

Oh, boy. That possibility hadn't even occurred to Eddie.

Extension 711 was busy. "Will you hold?" asked the operator. Eddie held while Pop drummed his fingers.

Finally, "Marketing Department."

"This is Eddie Zitelli again. Has my dad come back yet?"

"No, he hasn't. I put a note on his desk, telling him to call you as soon as he walks into the office."

Looking at Pop, Eddie knew that wasn't good

124

enough. "Is there any way to reach my dad where he is now? It's important that I talk to him."

"I could call Baker and Bradley, the office he's visiting. Maybe I can reach him there."

"That would be great. Really great."

Eddie gave Pop the message. Pop hitched sideways in his chair. His mouth worked, his thumb jerked against the tabletop. Eddie wrapped up the lunch meat and screwed the top on the mustard jar. He fed Jake the ham from Pop's sandwich, put the pitcher of iced tea back in the refrigerator, and wiped off the counter. When the phone rang, Eddie snatched it off the hook.

"I'm sorry, Eddie, I couldn't reach your dad. His meeting ran so long that he and the client went out to lunch. But the secretary at Baker and Bradley said your dad is headed back here after lunch. I'll have him call the minute he comes in the door."

Eddie hung up, dreading Pop's reaction to this news. "Listen, Pop—"

But Pop had already guessed. "I can't wait no longer, Eddie."

"You have to, Pop. What else can you do?" A lump began to form in Eddie's stomach because he knew what Pop's answer would be.

"I'm gonna drive to the track myself."

Chapter 15

"Come on, Pop. You can't drive to the track."

"I got a car, don't I? I got keys."

"I can't let you do it."

"You can't let me? I'm some kind of baby, you're gonna tell me what I can and can't do?" Pop pushed himself up from the table, his face purple, his mouth twisted into a scowl. "Outta my way, Eddie. I'm going."

It was Del Monte Street all over again. But this time Eddie had to stop Pop.

Then Pop held up his hand, the anger draining from his face. "Eddie, sometimes in life a person has to do something. Today I gotta go to the track."

The sudden change knocked Eddie off balance, as if he'd been braced against a stiff wind and the wind had died abruptly. Why didn't the phone ring, so he could hand this problem over to Dad? But the phone stayed silent. Mom was an hour away, and Eddie couldn't reach Tony. Eddie was on his own to deal with this one.

Sure as ducks had feathers, Pop was going to walk out that door and drive to the racetrack. Short of tying Pop to a bedpost, Eddie couldn't see any way to stop him. Well, let him go! It's not my problem, Eddie thought angrily. And for a moment felt relieved, as if he'd tipped an enormous weight off his shoulders.

But he couldn't do it. Eddie's life and Pop's had joined together these past weeks, like the branches of two trees growing side by side. Eddie couldn't just stand back and let Pop go off on his own.

Pop was waiting for Eddie's reaction. Eddie said the only thing he could say: "Pop, I'll go with you. Just let me leave Dad a note." Relief filled Pop's face like water rising in a pitcher, and Eddie knew that Pop had been hoping for that answer.

Eddie ripped the top page from the notepad and wrote on the fresh sheet: "Dad—Pop has to go to the racetrack. I couldn't reach you at the office, and I don't want Pop to go alone. So I'm going with him. Eddie." He hesitated, working his tongue across his retainer, then added: "I tried to stop him, but I couldn't." He left the pad in the middle of the table.

In the car, Pop muttered, "I don't know the way to the track from here. You got to help me."

How would Eddie know the route to the racetrack? "You got a map?"

"Eddie, I ain't driven this car much lately. I dunno what's in the glove compartment."

Great. He was riding with an eighty-three-year-old man who barely knew his own car. Eddie rifled the glove compartment and found a map of New Jersey. He unfolded it and studied the network of colored lines. "Okay, Pop, here's what we do. Wait a minute, you got gas?"

Pop squinted at the gas gauge and grinned triumphantly. "Practically full." He gunned the motor, and the Chevy bucked down the drive.

With Eddie navigating, Pop reached the highway and turned south. Traffic was heavy, and Pop, who had driven with confidence on the crowded streets of Philadelphia, suddenly turned jumpy as a long-tailed cat in a room full of rocking chairs. Hunched over the wheel, elbows stiff, he held the Chevy at forty-five while other cars whooshed past. Once a tractor trailer rumbled up behind and gave Pop the horn. Startled, Pop jerked the Chevy toward the shoulder, and the tires spat gravel. Pop wrenched the wheel the other way, and the car swerved back onto the highway.

Finally Eddie saw a sign that said racetrack. "There it is, Pop." Another sign followed: CLUBHOUSE AND VALET USE THIS GATE. Pop snapped the turn signal. The Chevy pulled across the line of oncoming traffic and plowed between the red brick pillars that marked the track entrance.

In the parking lot, rows of cars gleamed, shiny as beetles under the glittering sun. But Pop ignored the lot and drove straight to the clubhouse entrance. An attendant opened his door. "Park your car, sir?" Pop nodded and got out.

They'd made it. In one piece. Letting out a hard breath, Eddie scrambled from the car.

Pop bought tickets at the ticket booth and led Eddie through a grassy courtyard into the clubhouse lobby. "I'm gonna get me a program, Eddie."

Waiting for Pop, Eddie stared at the people milling in the lobby. Tanned men wearing sports jackets and pleated slacks. Guys in sunglasses and flowered shirts. Guys in T-shirts that barely covered their bulging bellies. Women in flat sandals and tight polyester pants; others teetering on high heels, their eyelashes thick with mascara, bracelets jangling on their wrists. And young people, mostly dressed in jeans and sneakers. Everybody was studying racing forms as though they were cramming for a final exam.

"Eddie—" Pop beckoned, and Eddie followed him through double doors into the betting room. Eddie's eyes slid along the island of grilled windows in the center of the room, each marked TELLER. One window carried a special sign: $50 MINIMUM WAGER PER TICKET. Imagine betting fifty bucks on a horse!

"I got to get my bearings. . . ." Pop craned his neck like an old snapping turtle. "Okay, we go this way." With Eddie behind him, Pop maneuvered toward the open doors at the end of the room.

Outside, under a bright blue sky, tiers of high-back benches sloped toward the racetrack. A truck was passing in front of the stands, misting the surface of the track with a spray of water. Behind the truck, a tractor dragged a rake that etched the dirt with fine grooves.

Pop touched Eddie's arm. "I got to sit down."

"You feeling okay?"

Pop settled onto an empty bench and grinned sideways at Eddie. "Excitement, that's all." Sunlight danced on Pop's spectacles and picked out a patch of stubble on his chin that he'd missed when he shaved.

Eddie grinned back, relief filling his chest. "Yeah, Pop."

Pop opened the racing form. His head close to Pop's, Eddie studied the list of horses for the third race. "There she is, Pop—Tia Two-Step."

"So she's really gonna run," Pop muttered. "That's okay, then."

Why wouldn't the horse run? But Pop was turning back to the first race. "Read the tote board for me, Eddie. Tell me the odds on the four horse. That's Mama's Boys."

Eddie studied the blinking numbers on the signboard opposite the grandstand. "Three to one. That's not what the newspaper said."

"Odds change right up to race time. Depends how the betting goes. But with this horse, I don't care about the odds. For Mama Z, I'm gonna bet two bucks. Come on."

Back inside, Pop placed his bet at a teller's cage. The teller punched buttons, and a paper ticket slid out. Pop waved the ticket at Eddie. "We got a winner. Guaranteed!"

A fanfare of trumpet notes sounded the call to racing. The silver music shivered up Eddie's spine. Maybe Pop did have a winner.

"C'mon, Eddie, we go see the horses."

Leaning over the fence at the end of the clubhouse area, Pop and Eddie watched the thoroughbreds come up the ramp from under the grandstand, passing so close that Eddie could have touched their thick manes and glossy flanks. The jockeys, splendid in crayon-colored silks and peaked caps, perched high up on the big horses, leather boots tucked into the short stirrups.

Out on the track other horses waited to meet the thoroughbreds, bearing riders dressed in jeans and hard hats. "Outriders," Pop explained. "They make sure all the horses get into the starting gate."

Pop and Eddie went back to the benches. They had barely sat down when the loudspeaker said: "The horses have reached the starting gate. And they're off! It's War Flag in the lead, Misty Bid second, Roman Fever outside at third, Mama's Boys fourth . . ."

Fourth! Eddie leaned forward, watching intently.

The horses vanished behind the tote board, then reappeared, with the announcer's voice continuing its rapid commentary: "At the far curve it's War Flag in the lead, Mama's Boys taking second . . ."

"She's moving!" Pop cried.

"Come on Mama's Boys!" shouted Eddie. Around the final turn . . . into the homestretch. Now the two lead horses were neck and neck. "Come on, Mama's Boys!" Eddie roared again, pounding on the bench.

132

The four horse moved ahead, opened up a lead, and thundered under the wire in first place.

"What did I tell you?" Pop held up his ticket, his face jubilant. "We got a winner!"

Elated, Eddie watched Pop scoop up his winnings at the ticket window. Then Pop turned toward the straight chairs that lined the wall.

"Sit down," Pop told Eddie. He took Eddie's hand and pressed into it the money he'd just won. "For you, Eddie. From Mama Z. At the racetrack, you got to have a couple of dollars in your pocket."

"No, Pop—"

Firmly Pop closed Eddie's fingers around the bills. "I don't want no arguments. You're bringin' me luck. Now listen, I'm not gonna bet the second race. I'll sit here, rest a little. You go out to the paddock, watch the horses line up for the race. When they bring out Tia Two-Step, look her over good."

"What am I looking for, Pop?"

"Make sure the horse has four legs, and the jockey ain't wearing dark glasses and carrying a tin cup. Before you go, buy us a soda. With all this shouting, my mouth is dry."

Waiting for two sodas at the snack-bar counter, Eddie nervously pleated the bills Pop had given him. He looked at Pop, wedged back in his chair, his short legs barely reaching the floor, and felt a rush of affection for his grandfather. But that feeling was followed by a cold draft of doubt. Pop figured Eddie was bringing him luck. Maybe. But what kind?

Chapter 16

Eddie went out the door to the paddock. Around the fenced ring, tall trees cast pools of shadow on bright green grass. People sat on benches beneath the trees or leaned on the fence around the ring. To Eddie's right, numbered stalls, all empty, occupied the base of the grandstand. A fenced pathway connected the stalls to the paddock.

I got to get my bearings. Yeah, Pop, thought Eddie, grinning. He swallowed the last of his soda and tossed the cup into a wire trash container.

An announcement crackled from a loudspeaker mounted on the grandstand wall: "It is now three minutes to post." At once, in the ring, a man's voice called, "Put your riders up please." Over the heads of the spectators lining the fence, Eddie saw the peaked caps of jockeys bob into view. A line of horses filed out of the paddock and disappeared into a tunnel under the grandstand.

Eddie figured those horses were headed out for the second race. That meant the horses for the third race would come next to the paddock. People were drifting toward the numbered stalls. Eddie headed toward stall eight, the number of Tia Two-Step's post position.

A tall man in a plaid sports shirt leaned on the fence beside a short guy with a sunburned nose. "I'm telling you, Harry," said the first man, shifting a toothpick in his mouth, "the four horse is hot."

"That horse will never do it, Sid. He's carryin' too much weight. I want you to see this eight horse. She looks good."

Eddie grinned. Right, Harry. Forget the four horse. Tia Two-Step was going to win this race.

A groom led a horse from the tunnel under the grandstand and entered stall number one. A second horse followed, then a third. Finally a sandy-haired groom approached stall eight. He led a sleek black horse with long slender legs and smoothly muscled flanks.

"That horse was made to run," Harry said admiringly, and Eddie felt his heart pump faster.

A stocky man wearing a pin-striped suit and a white dress shirt open at the neck entered the stall. He spoke to the groom and ran his hands approvingly over Tia Two-Step's glossy neck, a gold ring glittering on his pinkie. The horse's owner, Eddie decided.

Other people entered the stall: a man in a navy blue blazer carrying a clipboard, an attendant who brought

136

a blanket marked number eight, and a second groom who helped saddle Tia Two-Step.

As soon as the horses were saddled, they emerged from the stalls, led by their grooms and accompanied by their owners, and moved down the fenced lane to the paddock. When Tia Two-Step joined the parade, Eddie hurried over to the ring.

The jockeys were waiting, bright as tropical birds in their racing silks. Tia Two-Step's jockey, clad in emerald green and gold, shook hands with the man in the pin-striped suit. Tia Two-Step stood beside them, still as a statue.

What a gorgeous horse! Black as licorice, black as ebony. Even Eddie could see that Tia Two-Step was a winner. Noticing Harry and Sid at the fence, Eddie moved closer to listen to their conversation.

"You'll be throwin' money down the toilet," said Sid, the toothpick jiggling in his mouth. "That eight horse is a loser. Hasn't won a race since they brought her up from Bolivia last spring."

Eddie's fingers tightened on the fence rail. He waited for Harry to argue. But Harry only unwrapped a stick of gum and folded it into his mouth, still studying the black mare.

Cool it! Eddie told himself. Hadn't Pop said sometimes a horse was held back and on the right day the jockey would turn her loose? Yeah . . . but what if Tia Two-Step wasn't in the mood to run. What if she *liked* moving slow?

Eddie's eyes slid to the four horse, Sid's favorite.

A big chestnut-colored thoroughbred that jerked his head and danced on his hooves as if he had too much energy to stay still. He's carrying too much weight, Harry had told Sid. That horse didn't look as if a few extra pounds would slow him down.

Eddie's gaze came back to Tia Two-Step, motionless as a lump of coal. Maybe Tia Two-Step was saving her energy for the race. Maybe. Doubt flapped through Eddie's chest.

"Three minutes to post," crackled the loudspeaker, and the man in the blue blazer called out: "Put your riders up please." The grooms gave the jockeys a boost, and the horses filed toward the exit.

Eddie hurried back to Pop. "The horse looks okay?" Pop's eyes bored into Eddie's.

Eddie pushed down his doubts. "She's gorgeous, Pop. Like a stick of dynamite ready to explode."

"Tell me the odds. On that screen, Eddie."

Eddie studied the TV monitor mounted on a nearby column. "Eight horse . . . win column says twelve to one."

Pop struggled to his feet. "I got to place my bet. Stand in front of me."

Pop tugged his sports shirt and cotton undershirt out of the waistband of his slacks while Eddie watched, baffled. Pop fumbled beneath the undershirt and pulled out a creased envelope. Then he turned toward the betting windows.

"Hold it, Pop! You're headed for the fifty-dollar window."

Ignoring Eddie, Pop marched to the grilled window marked $50 MINIMUM WAGER PER TICKET and laid the envelope in front of the teller. "I want to put eighty-four hundred dollars on number eight to win," Pop said firmly.

Eddie's eyes flew wide.

Pop opened the envelope and took out a wad of bills held by a rubber band. Dumbfounded, Eddie stared as the teller pulled off the rubber band, licked his thumb, and began to count the crumpled bills. Where in blazes had Pop gotten $8,400?

The answer flashed inside Eddie's head. In the cellar of the house on Del Monte Street, that's where. Now Eddie knew why Pop had insisted on climbing down that rickety stairway. To find this envelope, tucked away in a hiding place in the dusty cellar.

The teller counted off crumpled tens, twenties, occasional fifties. Watching, Eddie realized where the money had come from. Doing without movies or trips to the seashore, walking instead of riding the bus, wearing the same clothes, tucking away a dollar here and a dollar there during the long years Pop was cutting hair in his barbershop. Pop had a modest income from the barbershop, plus Social Security—but Eddie was willing to bet that this money was his biggest chunk of extra cash. Eddie's mouth suddenly went dry. What if Tia Two-Step didn't win the race?

The teller recorded Pop's bet, and the ticket popped from the machine. Pop read the slip of paper carefully, then pushed it deep into his pocket. "Let's go, Eddie."

Seated on a bench close to the track, Pop turned to Eddie. "Tell me the odds now," he said. A blue vein pulsed in his forehead.

"Ten—" Eddie's voice cracked. "Ten to one, Pop." The odds had dropped, but ten times $8,400 was still enough to put in a first-floor bathroom and pay Vito's niece to cook and do the laundry. Enough for Pop to return to Del Monte Street.

The horses came up the ramp and filed onto the track. Eddie moistened his dry lips. "Look, Pop. The black horse is Tia Two-Step. Doesn't she look great?"

The tote board blinked, and the odds for Tia Two-Step dropped to nine to one. No more changes! Eddie protested. Don't let Pop's prize dwindle like soapsuds.

You're bringing me luck, Pop had told Eddie. Abruptly Eddie stood up. "Pop, I'll be back in a minute."

Eddie hurried inside, fishing out the bills that remained from the winnings Pop had given him. He stopped, studying the betting windows. He hadn't seen any kids his age at those windows. Maybe kids weren't allowed to place bets.

Harry and Sid stood before a TV monitor, eating hot dogs. Eddie walked up to them, his heart banging like a loose shutter. "Excuse me. Could you do me a favor?"

Harry wiped mustard from his mouth. "Whatta you have in mind, kid?"

"My grandfather wanted to bet on this race, but he

didn't feel like walking inside. Could you place a bet for him?"

"What's your grandfather's pleasure?"

"Four dollars on number eight to win."

Harry gave his hot dog to Sid and held out his hand. Eddie laid the four dollars on his palm.

Harry returned with two tickets, his yellow teeth showing in a smile. "That horse looks good to me too, kid. I'll give number eight a shot along with your grand-dad."

"Thanks!" Eddie croaked.

When Eddie showed Pop his ticket, Pop gave him a crooked grin. "You and me, Eddie, we're gonna be winners together."

Eddie hoped so. If he had any luck coming to him, Eddie hoped it would push Pop's luck along. But as he watched the outriders work the thoroughbreds into the starting gate, more doubts flapped in Eddie's chest.

The man sitting on Eddie's left cupped his hands to his mouth: "Keep him inside, Number Four, and you got it made! Piece of cake." Eddie's stomach churned. The four horse again. Four horse, eight horse . . . how could anyone know which horse would win?

"They're off!"

Eddie leaped to his feet as the horses exploded from the starting gate. The announcer's staccato voice moved as fast as the horses: "It's Scarlet Hiway in the lead . . . Dainty Dancer second."

Scarlet Hiway was the four horse, Sid's choice. Where was Tia Two-Step?

"My Goodness holds the inside at third . . . Maiden Lady fourth . . . Carlo Comeback fifth . . . "

The horses rounded the curve, and the announcer's voice rushed on: "Scarlet Hiway in the lead . . . My Goodness at second . . . Dainty Dancer third . . . Maiden Lady fourth . . . Tia Two-Step fifth . . ."

Fifth! The stupid horse was barely in the race.

"Coming down the backstretch, it's Scarlet Hiway in the lead . . . My Goodness holding second . . . Maiden Lady third . . . Tia Two-Step moving up on the outside . . ."

"Come on, Tia Two-Step!" Eddie shouted.

"Heading into the turn, Scarlet Hiway leads—just a minute—there's a rider down!" Panic clawed at Eddie's throat as he strained to see what was happening. "Maiden Lady is down and Tia Two-Step has moved up to third."

Tia Two-Step hadn't fallen. She'd moved to third place! Eddie whooped aloud, clutching Pop's arm.

"At the final turn it's Scarlet Hiway holding on at first . . . Tia Two-Step in second . . ." The horses spilled toward the finish line, hooves pounding. "Coming into the stretch, it's Scarlet Hiway the lead with Tia Two-Step moving up . . ."

The black horse and the chestnut were side by side! "Come on!" whooped Eddie, his heart thundering as the black horse edged in front. The horses shot past the wire. "Tia Two-Step is the winner!" roared the loudspeaker.

"She did it, Pop! She won!" Eddie crushed Pop in

a bear hug, and Pop's rusty laughter vibrated in Eddie's ears. They rocked together, laughing, thumping each other, fireworks of joy exploding in Eddie's chest.

Without warning, Pop's body sagged as if the bones in his legs had suddenly gone soft. Eddie staggered, catching Pop's weight in his arms. He lowered Pop onto the bench. Bracing Pop with one hand, Eddie lifted Pop's chin. Pop's face was sallow, his lips pale. Behind his bifocals, the whites of his eyes showed in bluish crescents beneath his drooping eyelids.

"Pop . . ." Eddie's voice was hoarse with terror.

"Old man's sick," someone said. "Call a guard."

A fierce wind roared inside Eddie's head, almost drowning out the voice from the loudspeaker: "Hold your tickets, ladies and gentlemen. An objection has been raised. . . ."

Chapter 17

"Coming through. Folks, let me through please." A freckled hand touched Eddie's shoulder, and Eddie looked up to see a husky red-haired man beside him with a wheelchair. "This your grandfather?"

Eddie nodded, his throat too tight for speech.

"Okay, son, you just slide over . . ." The guard placed his big hands under Pop's arms and lifted Pop into the wheelchair as easily as if Pop were a doll. He fastened a strap around Pop's chest and placed his feet on the footrest. Pop's head rolled back, and Eddie saw a trickle of saliva at the corner of his mouth. "Come with me," the guard told Eddie.

Behind a door marked FIRST AID, a plump black nurse in a white pantsuit clasped Pop's wrist between her fingers. The creases in her round face deepened as she checked Pop's pulse against her watch. "Oh my.

We want to get this nice gentleman to the hospital right away."

She spoke into the phone while Eddie sat, frozen, on a stiff-backed chair. Then the nurse said, "You have a mama or a daddy you want to call?"

Hope flared in Eddie's chest. Maybe Dad or Mom was home by now, ready to lift this awful responsibility from his shoulders. But the phone rang and rang, and no one answered.

As Eddie set the receiver back in the cradle, double doors in the wall bumped open, and two men rolled a stretcher into the room. With practiced skill, they transferred Pop to the stretcher.

"Come along, sugar." The nurse touched Eddie's arm. They followed the men to the front of the clubhouse where a cream-colored ambulance waited, its red light flashing.

"Eddie!"

Eddie jerked around. Dad was hurrying toward him, his suit jacket flapping. "What happened, Eddie?"

"Pop's sick." The words scraped Eddie's throat like ground glass, and tears burned his eyes.

"Could be a stroke," said the nurse. "Or a heart attack."

"Let me get my car," Dad told the ambulance driver. "I'll follow you to the hospital."

The world blurred as Eddie sprinted with Dad across the cinder parking lot. He heard the engine hum to life, felt the car skid into place behind the ambulance, listened to the thin whine of the siren as both vehicles shot out the gate onto the highway.

"What happened?" Dad repeated.

"I don't know. One minute Pop was fine, then all of a sudden his legs folded up and he couldn't talk." The terror of that moment flooded back.

"I called from the office. Mrs. Larrabee told me you sounded upset. When you didn't answer the phone, I drove home and found your note." The ambulance passed through a red light, siren squealing. Dad jammed the gas pedal down and followed. "What got into Pop? Why did he insist on going to the track today?"

"Somebody phoned this morning to give Pop a tip on a race. Pop wanted to go to the track so he could bet on the horse. When the secretary couldn't reach you, Pop said he was going alone." Eddie jammed his hands between his knees and sucked in a shuddering breath. "I couldn't get him to change his mind, so I came along."

The ambulance swung into the hospital parking lot and halted at a ramp marked EMERGENCY ONLY. Dad pulled into a parking spot, and he and Eddie sprang from the car.

The attendants wheeled the stretcher up the ramp and through a pair of heavy doors with Dad and Eddie following. Eddie felt a wave of cool air; his sneakers squeaked on the tile floor. The attendants maneuvered the stretcher through an archway into a curtained alcove. "Over here," said a nurse, directing Dad toward a counter.

While Dad was filling out admission forms, a second nurse appeared. "It will be a while before the doctor knows anything, Mr. Zitelli. You can wait down the hall."

They reached the waiting room, and Dad said, "I'll find a phone and call Mom." Eddie hunched in one of the stiff chairs, elbows digging into his knees. Let Pop come out of this okay. Please.

Dad returned. "Mom's on the way," he said, settling into the chair next to Eddie's. He tugged his lower lip between his fingers, a gesture so much like Pop's that Eddie's heart cracked.

They waited for a long time. Elevator doors hissed open and shut. People passed—hospital attendants in crepe-soled shoes rolling metal carts or carrying clipboards, visitors with potted plants, a teenager chewing gum. Finally a man in green hospital garb came toward them. "Mr. Zitelli? I'm Dr. Kennedy." Dad stood up, and the doctor spoke to him in low tones.

Dad returned to Eddie, his thick eyebrows knitted. "Pop had another stroke."

"Will he be okay?"

"The doctor doesn't know yet—they have to do more tests. He said I can see Pop before they start."

Eddie began to rise, but Dad shook his head. "Just me, Eddie."

Eddie leaned back in the chair. The vinyl upholstery chilled him through his thin shirt. He rubbed his hands along the wooden arms, remembering the feel of Pop's knobby shoulders as he and Pop jigged together in that joyous moment before the wires holding Pop together snapped.

A woman approached the elevators, pushing her hair back from her face as she studied the directory on the wall. Mom. Eddie started up from his chair, but just then the elevator door opened and Dad came out. Eddie watched them, Mom's head tilted forward, her face pale and thoughtful, Dad's shoulders hunched in a gesture that said he didn't know, he didn't know.

They came across the waiting room, and his mother laid the back of her hand against Eddie's cheek. Hot tears burned behind his eyelids. "Beanie was at our house looking for you when Dad called," Mom said. "Beanie phoned his father, and Mr. Beane offered to drive me down. He's waiting outside to take you home."

"I want to stay with you and Dad."

"There won't be any news till the tests are finished," Dad said. "It may be a long time." His set face left no room for argument.

Mr. Beane saw Eddie coming and leaned over to open the van door. "I'm sorry about your grandfather," he said. And that was all. Eddie was glad of Mr. Beane's silence, glad to let the odors of paint and turpentine and the steady rumble of the van take up all the space in his head.

Back in Belvidere, the van bumped up the driveway and halted. "If we can do anything, give Beanie a call. You hear, Eddie? Anything at all."

Eddie thanked Mr. Beane and mounted the breezeway steps. Mickey flung the door back, her eyes round as full moons. "Is Pop okay?"

"What happened?" Tony burst through the basement doorway. "Mickey told me this crazy story about you and Pop going to the races and Pop ending up in the hospital."

"That's right."

"You let Pop drive that old Chevy to the racetrack? Eddie, when God gave out brains you were under the bed. What's the matter with Pop?"

"He had another stroke."

"Bad?"

"I don't know." Eddie thrust out his arms. "I don't know!"

He strode past Tony and Mickey and ran to his bedroom. He flung himself across the bed, fists knotted against his temples, a gust of wind whirling inside his head.

Eddie woke with a start, his lips stiff and cracked. He stumbled to the kitchen and found Tony and Mickey at the table, a pizza and a half-liter of Coke between them.

"What time is it?"

"Almost nine. Mickey was hungry, so I ordered pizza. Enough for you too."

"Any word?"

Tony shook his head.

Eddie pulled out a chair. He looked at the oily cheese covering the pizza, and his stomach contracted.

"Eddie, what happened? Tell me from the beginning."

"Pop and I went to the racetrack."

"Sure. Pop just said, 'Hey, Eddie, let's take a little spin down to the track,' and away you went. There's more to it than that."

Eddie poured soda into a glass and drank it down. The cold liquid gurgled in his stomach. "Some guy called and gave Pop a tip on a horse—that's why he wanted to go to the track. When I couldn't reach Dad, Pop insisted he was going anyway. So I went with him."

Tony's eyes sharpened with curiosity. "Did Pop bet on the horse?"

The question bounced inside Eddie's head like a tennis ball. He'd forgotten all about the stupid race.

"Yeah. And the horse won. But Pop collapsed right after the race. Then something else happened." Eddie pressed his fingers to his forehead, remembering. "The loudspeaker said something about an objection and people should hang on to their tickets. That's all I know."

"Where's Pop's ticket?"

"In his pocket. Wait a minute, I bet on the same horse." Eddie fished out the bit of paper and handed it to Tony.

"How much did Pop bet?"

"Eighty-four hundred dollars."

Tony's jaw dropped. "You're kidding! Where did Pop find that kind of dough? What were the odds on this horse?"

"Nine to one."

"Nine to one!" Tony shoved back his chair and

reached for the phone. "Information? I want the number for the Atlantic City Racetrack. Yeah, the line that gives out race results." He covered the receiver, staring at Eddie. "Do you realize what this means? If that horse won, Pop has over seventy thousand dollars coming to him." Tony listened to the phone number, nodding, then hung up.

Eddie reached for the phone. "You place the call. I'll listen to the message."

Tony hesitated, then handed the receiver to Eddie.

Eddie's chest tightened as he waited for Tony to press the number. That bit of paper tucked inside Pop's pocket was his ticket to Del Monte Street. Eddie saw again the flashing black forelegs of Tia Two-Step and heard the announcer's warning: "Hold your tickets, ladies and gentlemen . . ."

A recorded voice droned in Eddie's ear: "Here are today's race results." Eddie waited, the pressure building in his chest, as the voice went through the first two races. Then: "In the third race . . ."

The announcement ended, and Eddie set the receiver gently back on the hook.

"Well?"

"Pop's horse was scratched for interference."

"What does that mean?" piped Mickey.

"The horse was disqualified," Tony said flatly. "Put out of the race. Pop wanted that money to help him go home to Del Monte Street, didn't he? Hey, Eddie, I'm talking to you! Why didn't you stop Pop from gambling all that money? Pop didn't need any more bad luck."

152

Eddie's head flew up. "Shut up, Tony!"

"Who you telling to shut up?"

"You. Keep quiet. Button your lip."

"You gonna make me?"

Eddie slammed his hands against Tony's chest. Tony's head jerked back, and his eyes narrowed.

"You want to play rough? Okay, I'll play rough." In one swift movement Tony hooked his foot behind Eddie's ankles and shoved. Eddie staggered and sprawled backward onto the floor with Tony on top of him, his knees pinning Eddie's arms.

On top. Where Tony always wound up.

A scarlet film flowed across Eddie's eyes, and he wrenched one arm free, heaving his hips up at the same time. Tony lurched against the refrigerator. Eddie struggled onto his side, spilling Tony off, and they rolled over, grappling for a hold. Then Tony flung his leg across Eddie's thigh and pulled himself back onto Eddie's stomach. He leaned close to Eddie, perspiration shiny on his forehead. "Give up?" he panted.

Tony's weight was crushing Eddie. He heard a car door slam as he gasped, "I give."

Tony grabbed the handle on the refrigerator door and pulled himself up. Eddie stumbled to his feet facing Tony, their eyes dead level.

Then Mom and Dad came through the breezeway door. Eddie saw the shadows under Mom's eyes, the deep creases in his father's cheeks, and knew at once, knew before Dad stumbled over the hard words, that Pop would never go home to Del Monte Street.

153

Chapter 18

Sometime during the night Eddie started up in bed. Staring into darkness, he strained to hear the sound that had awakened him. Crickets droned through the open window, leaves stirred in the soft night air. Nothing else. No ragged breathing, no click of false teeth from across the room.

Pop didn't need any more bad luck.

Shut up, Tony. Shut up.

In the morning, waking came hard. Eddie struggled toward the surface like a swimmer pushing up through deep water. When he opened his eyes and saw the flat, smooth bed across the room, pain sharp as thorns raked his chest.

Aunt Tess and her family drove from Ohio for the funeral, Aunt Tess clumsily pregnant, her voice catching as she spoke of the grandchild Pop and Mama Z would never see. Father Charles didn't make the trip.

He'd flown up from Brazil nine months earlier when Mama Z died, and the airfare was too costly for him to return. "Don't even consider it, Charlie," Dad had said on the phone. "Pop would understand." Eddie heard the raw edge in his father's voice, and his own throat ached.

Instead of a viewing, friends were invited to call at St. Agnes Church on the morning of the funeral. Mama Z's was the only other funeral Eddie had attended, here in this same church with its carved wooden pews and marble floor. While Mom and Dad approached the casket with Mickey between them, Eddie waited beside Tony. He balled his fists and felt the sleeves of Tony's hand-me-down sports jacket, too short in the sleeves, rub against his wrists. Then Tony nudged him, and Eddie walked with Tony to kneel beside the casket.

The fragance of hothouse flowers surrounded Eddie as he looked at the still figure in the casket. Dark gray suit, white dress shirt, silver-striped tie. Pop hated ties. Eddie wished he could loosen that stiff knot and hear Pop whisper, "That's better. Yeah, that's better." Eddie's eyes shifted to Pop's face. Behind his steel-rimmed bifocals, Pop's crumpled eyelids were closed. His usually fuzzy hair was smooth, combed flat across his head.

Eddie waited for the ache in his chest to overflow. Instead an odd thing happened. The longer Eddie looked at the still figure in the casket, the less he recognized Pop.

In late summer Eddie had sometimes found empty

cicada shells, brittle as dry leaves, clinging to tree trunks in the backyard. That's what this figure reminded him of, a shell Pop had discarded. Corky Zitelli, Eddie's grandfather who once climbed a cable into the blue sky over Brooklyn, had vanished.

Tony touched his forehead, beginning the sign of the cross. Eddie stole a sideways glance at his brother's calm profile. He didn't understand Tony. Pop's best buddy—but Tony had walked dry-eyed through these painful days.

Not Mickey. As they headed back to join their parents in the pew, Eddie saw that his sister was crying again, leaning against Mom, while Mom stroked her thumb across Mickey's wet cheek. No tears, Eddie ordered himself fiercely. He had cried plenty that first night alone in the bedroom, but the tears hadn't helped, hadn't softened the jagged lump he carried in his chest.

After the funeral mass, family and friends drove to the cemetery where broad, green-leafed trees cast islands of shadow on the soft grass. The priest intoned the final prayers and, one by one, family members laid white carnations on Pop's casket.

Then they returned to the house on Del Monte Street where neighbors had set out platters of food: lunch meat and cheese, potato salad and coleslaw, baskets of rolls, and cakes thick with frosting. Eddie followed Tony around the dining room table, serving himself food he didn't want. Tony, his plate piled high,

157

went through the kitchen door. Eddie saw him pull out a chair at the table beside their cousins Lisa and Joey, and saw the laughter that sprang to Lisa's eyes at Tony's first comment.

Eddie headed instead for the second floor. Turning away from the buzz of voices in the living room, he went into Pop and Mama Z's silent, empty bedroom. On the far side of Pop's bureau he sat down on the floor, the plate of food beside him. Arms wrapped around his knees, Eddie watched the lace curtains at the open window stir in the breeze, letting in the scent of city heat.

Then floorboards creaked. "Next week for sure," said Dad's voice.

"Whenever you're ready, Don. Take your time." That was Joe Salvatore. He and Dad stood together, just inside the bedroom door.

"Tess and I are glad you want to buy the business, Joe. And the house. Pop would be pleased to know your family's living here."

"Corky was a good man, a good barber. Taught me everything I know."

"Pop wanted to come home so badly. But he couldn't have managed here on his own, not even with help. Sooner or later, he had to face that."

"This way he didn't have to face it, Don. Corky died believing he'd be able to come home again. That's not so bad, is it?"

The voices went away, and Eddie pressed his fore-

158

head against his knees. Pop died believing that Tia Two-Step had won the race, that with his winnings he'd be able to return to Del Monte Street. *That's not so bad, is it?* The pain that scraped the inside of Eddie's chest softened.

The next day rain fell in steady silver lines, soaking the lawn and making puddles around the roots of the maple tree. Tony's boss called to say Tony wouldn't be needed at work. Dad took the day off. He shut himself in the bedroom at the card table, a pile of papers spread before him.

After lunch, restless from being indoors, Eddie went out onto the breezeway. Jake slipped out beside him. When Eddie sat down, Jake rubbed against his ankles until Eddie picked the cat up. For a long time he held Jake against his chest, stroking the rough fur and feeling the cat's rumbling warmth. Finally Eddie went back inside.

In his bedroom Mom stood in front of the closet, slipping Pop's plaid shirt from its hanger. A pile of folded shirts lay on the end of the bed.

"What are you doing?" Eddie asked.

"Making room for Tony to move upstairs."

Outrage jammed Eddie's throat. "What's the hurry?"

"Dad needs his office, honey. With all the paperwork from Pop's affairs along with his own job, Dad needs his desk and filing cabinets."

"What will you do with Pop's clothes?"

His mother sighed. "Give them to the Salvation Army, I guess. Pop and Mama Z wouldn't want good clothes wasted."

A bunch of strangers pawing through Pop's clothes—Eddie hated the idea. "That plaid shirt. Can I have it?"

Wordlessly, his mother held out the folded shirt. Eddie put it in the bureau drawer with his own things. The shirt was too small for Eddie, but he couldn't let a stranger walk around in Mama Z's gift to Pop.

Mom watched him, rubbing her hands along her arms as if she felt cold. "Would you like anything else of Pop's?"

Eddie picked up the framed snapshot from Pop's bureau, the one Pop had brought back from Del Monte Street.

"Pop and Mama Z's fiftieth anniversary. That's a lovely picture to remember them by." Mom tipped her head sideways, her eyes turning soft. "You were right to go to the racetrack with Pop, Eddie. He would have driven there alone, Dad and I know that. You did everything you could for Pop. We all did. Sometimes strokes just happen, no matter how hard people try to prevent them." She turned to the closet and took Pop's striped pajamas from the hook on the door. "Why don't you look through the drawers, Eddie? See if there's anything else of Pop's you'd like to keep."

The top drawer held rolled socks, two coiled leather belts, Pop's change purse. Eddie picked up the purse, remembering the twenty dollar bill Pop had pulled from it to rescue Eddie. "I'd like this," he said and snapped the metal clasp open.

"Fine," said Mom.

Eddie glanced inside, and his heart stumbled to a halt.

Chapter 19

Eddie fled to the bathroom and closed the door. He opened the purse again, his fingers unsteady on the stiff clasp.

Oh Pop! Angrily Eddie stared at the pills in the bottom of the purse, yellow ones and brown, heaped up like tiny pebbles. How many times had Pop pretended to take his medicine, then hidden the pills in this purse, where he was sure Mom wouldn't discover them when she put away clean laundry?

Eddie sat down on the side of the bathtub. Maybe these pills would have kept Pop from having a second stroke. Maybe Pop would be alive now if he'd taken them. Knives of anger flashed inside Eddie's chest. Stubborn old man! What right did he have to refuse this medicine when everybody in the family was working so hard to help him get well?

"Eddie . . ." Mom's voice, outside the door. "Are you okay?"

Eddie leaped to his feet, ready to confront his mother with the evidence of Pop's treachery. He hesitated, his hand on the doorknob, remembering Pop's words. *Things you do in life, you got to take responsibility for them. That's what it means to be a man.* Pop had lived life the way he wanted, had made his own decisions right up to the end. Showing Mom these pills wouldn't bring Pop back, but it would destroy Mom's belief that she'd done everything possible to help Pop.

"Eddie?"

Eddie drew a hard breath. "I'm okay, Mom," he called. "I'm fine."

He spilled the pills into the toilet bowl and pressed the handle. As water whirled inside the bowl, sweeping the pills out of sight, Eddie could almost hear a rusty chuckle of approval from Pop.

Mom was waiting in the hall. She cupped Eddie's face between her palms and smoothed his eyebrows with the balls of her thumbs. "Why don't you help Tony carry his things upstairs?"

Down in the basement, Tony lay on the weight bench, doing pull-overs. When he saw Eddie on the stairs, he clanged the bar into the metal cradle and sat up. "Buzz off."

Eddie stared at Tony's puffy face and red-rimmed eyes. "You've been crying," he blurted.

"I said scram! Go on, Eddie."

"Because of Pop?"

"None of your business." Tony's face contracted, and he bent forward, pressing his forehead against the metal bar. "Yeah, because of Pop. Because I didn't spend more time with him while he was here."

"You were busy," Eddie said cautiously. "With baseball practice. Your job."

Tony looked at Eddie, his eyes dark holes. "I could have found time. I didn't want to."

"What do you mean?"

"I kept away on purpose because everybody says I'm the spitting image of Pop. I didn't want to think about that." Tony stood up, holding his arms out. "Look at me, Eddie!"

"What are you talking about? You look the same as always."

"Yeah. The way I looked last year and the year before that. I haven't grown an inch in two years. I used to be one of the tallest kids in my class. Now I'm one of the shortest. I'm going to be as short as Pop."

"Come on, Tony, you're only fourteen. You'll grow more."

"Who says?" Tony's voice was ragged. "You're two years younger, and already you've caught up with me!"

The truth shimmered into view like a photo developing from a negative. So that was why Tony had thrown a fit when he saw Eddie's fingerprints on the bedroom ceiling. And why Tony had been measuring himself against the door to the cedar closet. Not just so he could put up a chinning bar, but to see if he'd grown any taller.

Tony sat down, his face creased with pain, and Eddie felt a sudden wrench in his stomach. Tony had been hauling around a load of troubles, and Eddie had been so wrapped up in his own miseries that he hadn't even noticed.

Something pricked at the edge of Eddie's mind. He frowned, figuring out what it was. "Wait a minute, Tony," he called, scrambling up the stairs. "I'll be right back."

Eddie returned triumphant, holding out the snapshot from Pop's bureau. "Look . . . Father Charles, Dad, even Aunt Tess—they're all taller than Pop. Every one of Pop's kids grew bigger than he was. It stands to reason that his grandchildren will too."

Tony tilted the snapshot toward the light, studying it carefully. He shrugged, but Eddie saw a flicker of hope in his brother's eyes. "I don't know. Maybe you're right."

"I am. Tony, I know I'm right."

"Not much I can do about it, is there, but wait and see." Tony studied the photo again. His lips puffed out, and he said in a rush, "I wish I'd spent more time with Pop this summer."

"I'm glad you didn't." The words jumped out before Eddie had time to think what he was saying. "Maybe it's rotten for me to feel this way, but you and Pop were already buddies. This was the only chance I had to hang around with Pop."

"He was a hell of a guy, wasn't he? Pop took me to my first Phillies game, you know that? While we were sitting there, eating hot dogs, slurping down sodas, Pop told me Father Charles had scouts from three pro teams looking at him in high school. Pop figured Father Charles could have made it big in baseball if he hadn't entered the priesthood. And he said I was going to be even better than Father Charles. I'm not counting on that, but Pop made me feel so good that day. I'll never forget it."

Did Tony know about Pop's BB gun? Or the story of Pop's adventure on the Brooklyn Bridge? Some day Eddie would ask, but right now silence felt exactly right between him and Tony.

"Eddie!" Mickey's feet clattered on the stairs. "A package came. For you! You won some kind of prize."

"Hear that?" Tony rose and stepped over the weight bench. "Let's check it out."

He'd won a prize? Baffled, Eddie followed Tony up the stairs. The days when he'd figured all his problems could be solved by winning a contest seemed far away, like another life he could barely remember.

The carton by the front door was stamped with bright blue letters: CONGRATULATIONS! YOU'VE WON A PRIZE FROM FAIRCHILD FOODS. Mickey danced up and down beside it, eyes flashing.

"UPS brought it," said Mom. "Weighs a lot."

"There's a letter." Dad tapped the envelope glued to the top of the carton.

Eddie approached warily, as though the carton might contain TNT. He tore open the envelope and read aloud: "Dear Mr. Zitelli . . ."

"Mis-ter Zitelli? Hot stuff," teased Tony.

"Congratulations on winning sixty-ninth place in our EAT WELL, AMERICA contest. As your prize, we are pleased to send you a generous supply of one of our fine food products—" Eddie broke off, staring at the letter.

"Pretzels!" guessed Mickey.

Mom shook her head. "Carton weighs too much."

"Salted peanuts," said Dad.

"Chocolate bars."

"After-dinner mints!"

"Come on, Eddie—tell us!"

They stared at him, their faces alive with curiosity.

Eddie sat down heavily on the carton. "I won forty-eight boxes of dried prunes."

"Prunes." His mother put her hand to her mouth. "Oh my."

For a moment no one spoke. Then Tony cuffed Eddie's shoulder. "Hey! A prize is a prize."

Dad cleared his throat. "Sure it is. Just think, we can have stewed prunes for breakfast."

"I can make prune danish," Mom suggested.

Mickey giggled. "And pancakes with prune syrup."

"For lunch"—Tony grinned broadly— "how about peanut butter and prune sandwiches?"

"With prune pie for dessert."

"And prune-topped pizza for a snack!" Dad's face had turned crimson, and his mouth was quivering.

"I'll serve stuffed prunes to my card club," Mom spluttered. "Stuffed with—"

"More prunes!"

They were all laughing now, shoulders heaving, faces scarlet.

Amid the laughter, Dad put his arm around Eddie and lifted Eddie's hand into the air, like a referee announcing the outcome of a prizefight. "La-dies and gent-le-men, I give you our winner: Lucky Eddie Zitelli!"

Eddie felt Dad's arm on his shoulders, the warmth of Dad's hand holding his. He looked at his family surrounding him—Tony whistling, Mom clapping, Mickey jigging up and down. All of them cheering for Eddie.

Lucky Eddie.